# FLORA STORMER
## and the *Mystic Pearl*

**Illustrated by Hannah McCaffery**

*For my family.*
*When cast into troubled waters, we*
*are kept afloat by the stories we tell.*

ORCHARD BOOKS

First published in Great Britain in 2024 by Hodder & Stoughton

1 3 5 7 9 10 8 6 4 2

Text © Hodder & Stoughton Limited 2024
Cover and inside illustrations by Hannah McCaffery © Hodder & Stoughton
Limited 2024

A CIP catalogue record for this book is available from the British Library.

ISBN 978 1 40837 004 9

Printed in Great Britain

MIX
Paper | Supporting
responsible forestry
FSC    FSC® C104740
www.fsc.org

The paper and board used in this book are made from
wood from responsible sources

Orchard Books
An imprint of Hachette Children's Group
Part of Hodder & Stoughton Limited
Carmelite House, 50 Victoria Embankment, London EC4Y 0DZ

The authorised representative in the EEA is Hachette Ireland, 8 Castlecourt Centre,
Castleknock Road, Castleknock, Dublin 15, D15 YF6A, Ireland

An Hachette UK Company
www.hachette.co.uk
www.hachettechildrens.co.uk

# Contents

# Chapter One

"Are you ready? You're about to see some *marvellous* things!"

Flora's father could barely contain his excitement as he stood before Flora. Behind him was a pair of towering doors, the entrance to the Great Exhibition. "Now we must try not to get too distracted," he said, his gaze already wandering over the crowds around them. "We're here to support Pavan, after all."

Her father had told her all about the Great Exhibition, and now she was going to see it for herself! It was meant to be where all the greatest minds gathered to showcase their discoveries and inventions, and she was going to be in the middle of it all. She patted her bag containing her painting supplies, and felt a fizz of excitement at the thought of what she might paint that day.

"I wonder where Pavan's exhibit will be . . ." Flora started to say, but stopped when she realised her father had already wandered into the building. She laughed and ran in after him.

As soon as she entered, Flora was overwhelmed by a thousand noises, sights and smells. Everywhere they looked they saw incredible things! Beneath the high glass ceiling there were countless stalls, statues and exhibits. Some were displaying amazing and often bizarre inventions, others were advertising psychics and spiritualists who promised a peek into the afterlife, while here and there were stalls manned by eccentric people selling miracle cures that made Flora's nose wrinkle in disgust.

One cure, which a man in a top hat and large handlebar moustache was peddling as "a tonic for all illnesses, as well as a great household cleaner and sink unblocker", contained so many poisons that one whiff could knock anyone stone dead. *Which*, Flora thought, *is one way to cure an illness.*

They snaked their way through the crowds, their attention being pulled in every direction. Another stall caught their eye as it had gathered considerable interest; a large banner above it said "Leeches that can predict the weather!".

Beneath this bizarre banner was an ornate contraption made of wood, brass and glass, with twelve glass bottles that were positioned in a circle round the edge of it. A skinny man in a green suit and a purple top hat was hopping around in front of the odd machine.

"Oh, yes, ladies and gentlemen! You'd better believe it! When these leeches sense a storm is coming, they will crawl to the top of their bottles! Imagine, madam," he said, lurching towards a woman in the crowd, who stumbled backwards in alarm. "You too could harness nature's power in your own parlour!"

Flora bent down and saw that, yes, there were leeches inside each of the bottles! YUCK! And yet

. . . Flora couldn't help but feel a little sorry for those leeches, trapped and on display.

Suddenly, there was a terrified shriek. Startled, the crowd turned to see a woman standing beside two children, a guilty-looking little boy and a very small girl who was covered in leeches. The slug-like creatures were attached to every inch of her face!

"Oh, no, madam!" cried the stallholder, his purple top hat almost falling off his head as he rushed forward. "Those are the spare leeches! Please don't distract them or they'll lose their focus!"

"Flora! Over here!"

Flora looked away from the man in the green suit plucking leeches from the girl's face and caught sight of Pavan waving frantically. She

waved back with a grin and began pulling her father through the crowds towards him.

Pavan, who was a little older than Flora, was tall and skinny; in fact, he had grown several inches since leaving Lord Granville's employ to live with Flora and her father! He had travelled to England as an orphan from India, and was now proving his skills as the best inventor Flora had ever met.

He stood proudly in front of a huge glass jar filled to the brim with colourful jelly sweets, surrounded by interested onlookers. Above him was a bright sign that Flora had painted for him, displaying the words "A meal in every mouthful!".

As they approached, someone from the crowd called out. "Young sir, what is it we're looking at? A meal in every mouthful, what does that mean?"

Pavan beamed with pride. "I have made a machine that can compress food into a jelly-like substance. Just one of these sweets can provide the sustenance of an entire meal! I hope that we can use it to combat world hunger one day."

"An *entire* meal?" asked one woman, peering into the jar. "Does that mean it will taste like roast chicken and vegetables?"

"Not at all!" Pavan smiled, coming to the rescue with an explanation. "I've given them all fruity flavours."

Flora grimaced, remembering the early stages of Pavan's invention, when they were all sick for a week after "the haddock-flavoured incident".

One man nodded his head enthusiastically. "You must be very talented to invent something like this at such a young age," he said.

"Well, I . . ." Pavan hesitated, trailing off awkwardly.

"Yes, he is. He's a brilliant inventor," Flora said confidently. "His quick-thinking and mechanical know-how have saved the day more than once."

Pavan grinned at her praise.

"Any comment for the press?" came an official-sounding voice that Flora instantly recognised.

"Lavinia!" cried Flora and Pavan.

Lavinia laughed and hugged them both. It was so wonderful to see her! Since her success as an author following their adventure together on Isla Panacea, Lavinia had been very busy juggling her writing alongside her journalism career. Letting go of her friends, she ran her hand through her short blonde hair and straightened her suit jacket.

"What are you doing here?" asked Flora.

"I'm writing an article about the explorers trying to reach the North Pole first! It's all very exciting; there are three separate groups about to make the daring expedition, and they're all here trying to raise funds and awareness." She spotted somebody in the crowd and beckoned them over. "Dr Robinson, over here!"

A man broke through the barrier of people and shook Lavinia's hand. He had a long face that seemed almost carved out of stone, with a hard line for a mouth, piercing blue eyes and greying blonde hair. The overall effect was of somebody extremely serious.

"Dr Robinson is leading the dog-sled team," Lavinia told her friends. "I'm travelling with them to cover the expedition."

"How exciting," said Flora.

"Dr Robinson, these are my friends. Flora is a great illustrator and Pavan is the best inventor I know! He's here exhibiting one of his creations."

Dr Robinson said nothing but leant forward to inspect Pavan's jelly sweets. While he listened to Pavan's explanation, Lavinia leant over to Flora.

"Dr Robinson is very confident that he'll get to the North Pole before the other teams. But there's a hot-air balloon team also setting off. I'm hoping to interview the pilot."

"You seem like a good man to have in a tight spot," Dr Robinson said, putting an arm round Pavan.

"How would you like to join my team?"

Before Flora could hear Pavan's response, several more people moved forward to look at his invention, making Flora feel a little crowded. She turned to Lavinia, but before she could say anything she shook her head several times and clapped her hands. Flora called these kind of things tics; they were movements and sounds that she couldn't control. Lavinia nodded, understanding that Flora was feeling overwhelmed, but as she reached for her there was a loud announcement about the demonstration of a new money-printing machine.

The crowd began to surge round her, pushing her this way and that. Flora was lost in a sea of adults. She spun around, unable to see Pavan, Lavinia or her father, feeling like she was about to be trampled, when somebody lay a hand on her arm.

Flora turned to see a woman, bent over with age, her face hidden by a dark veil. She tried to pull her arm away, but the hand that gripped her was too strong and the gold rings on the woman's fingers dug into Flora's skin. Beneath the veil was an awful sound of rattling, ragged breathing.

"Your mother says to follow the whale," the woman said, her voice distant and unnatural. "Follow the whale . . ."

Flora gasped. Her mother died a long time ago when Flora was young. What could it mean?

The woman began to pull Flora towards a tent-like structure that was nestled between two stalls. It was odd that Flora hadn't noticed it before; it looked so out of place, with gauzy fabric hanging over it in shades of black, green and blue so it shimmered like a magpie's wing. Even more strangely, none of the passers-by in the immense crowd were giving the tent a single glance. It was as if their eyes just . . . slipped over it.

Flora looked behind her for Pavan, Lavinia or her father but could not see them. Still, she allowed herself to be led by the woman who had fuelled her curiosity. Had she really heard a message from her mother?

The veiled woman swept aside the fabric at the entrance with her other arm, which Flora noticed was missing a hand; her arm ended at the wrist. But soon her attention was pulled elsewhere, as together they entered the tent.

Flora wasn't sure what she had expected but it wasn't this. It was as if they had entered the parlour of a very fine lady, with heavy lace tablecloths, dark wooden furniture and large potted plants in every corner. There were red silk scarves draped over the lamps, which dimmed the light and gave it a rosy tint that somehow matched the heavy perfume that filled the air.

The woman led Flora to a table in the middle of the room and sat her in a tall wooden chair. She rang a small bell three times, then sat opposite Flora. Between them sat a large round ball on an ornate stand.

Was this a crystal ball? Flora had heard some spiritualists used them to contact the dead. But . . . weren't crystal balls meant to be see-through? This one had a pearly sheen to it and was certainly not made of crystal.

Finally, the woman lifted her veil. Her face was

lined and shrewd, her eyes sharply staring at Flora. Eyes that were a shimmering purple! Flora's heart started beating faster.

After a deep, rattling breath, the woman began to speak.

"You have always felt different to others. You lost your mother at a young age. You miss her. And you –" she raised her hand and pointed a finger at Flora – "you are the one who found the golden lotus."

Flora gasped. "How do you know that?"

The golden lotus was a magical flower that grew deep in the rainforest on Isla Panacea. When her

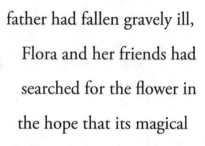

father had fallen gravely ill, Flora and her friends had searched for the flower in the hope that its magical healing properties would save his life. When they had found it, they had all promised to keep its existence a secret.

"There is something special about you," continued the spiritualist. "You have a connection with the natural world. You respect it, and it respects you. Because of this connection . . . I see magic flowing through you. You have been gifted a great deal."

It was true. Flora had experienced magic on Isla Panacea, which had opened her eyes to the power of nature. She had met the rainforest spirits who protected the rainforest and whose anger at its mistreatment had almost killed them all.

"BUT!" The woman threw up her arms, disturbing the silence. "You do not need to know your past. You need to know your future. I have been given a message for you. A warning."

She closed her eyes and began to chant words that Flora couldn't understand, raising and lowering her voice so that it fell in waves. The lights flickered and began to splutter, as a slight breeze crept around them. The breeze turned into a strong wind as the woman continued to chant, and it pulled at Flora's hair and whipped up the tablecloths and silk scarves, sending them flying into the air.

The spiritualist did not open her eyes, apparently unaware of the gale that had begun to rage inside the tent, while Flora gripped the table in fear.

The woman's voice became quieter, but she continued to chant. Flora closed her eyes and took a deep breath in, feeling herself shiver as the temperature dropped. The freezing wind stirred around her violently, and she began to feel little icy pinpricks across her skin . . . Were those snowflakes? It felt as if she were in the centre of a snowstorm! From behind her came the heavy padding footsteps of a large . . . animal . . .

Flora's eyes flew open and she turned quickly, her heart beating so fast she could hear it thudding. But there was nothing behind her except a flowery and rather squishy-looking armchair.

Turning back, Flora saw that the woman still had her eyes closed, but her hand was hovering over the crystal ball. Shapes were forming on the pearly surface, then flitting away before Flora could make them out.

"You will face great danger. There will be blood

and treachery. But there will also be new friends and great kindness. Your mother says to follow the whale . . ."

With that, she held something out to Flora. It was a small ivory-coloured wooden carving of a whale hanging on a black string necklace. Frowning, Flora took it.

As Flora's fingers touched the carving, she felt warm energy rising through her. A tiny sound, far off in the distance, made her lift her head, listening. The sound grew into the notes of a song, distant, echoing, full of sadness and just a little hope. It was the most beautiful music Flora had ever heard. She closed her eyes, listening to the rise and fall of the notes as they wound their way from some faraway place, feeling a shiver run through her.

"That's enough."

Lavinia's angry voice cut through the mystical atmosphere. Flora turned to see her at the entrance of the tent, a look of fury on her face. She strode in and put a hand on Flora's shoulder.

"Come on, we're leaving."

# Chapter Two

Lavinia steered Flora out of the tent and into the crowd with a fiery expression that kept everyone at bay.

"Wait . . ." Flora frantically looked over her shoulder at the woman in the veil, who was standing at the entrance of the tent. "She gave me a message from my mother!"

Lavinia guided Flora into a space between two

stalls, away from the moving people, and put both hands on her shoulders.

"Flora, that woman was a spiritualist. They're charlatans who prey on people's grief for money. They tell you whatever you want to hear and pretend it's a message from the afterlife. It wasn't a message from your mother."

Flora frowned, but seeing the concern in Lavinia's eyes she decided not to argue. In her heart, though, she wasn't so sure. After all, the spiritualist hadn't wanted any money. Hadn't she met the rainforest spirits on Isla Panacea? She knew first-hand that there was more to the world than meets the eye. Was it so far-fetched to think that her mother had sent her a message from the other side?

Lavinia led her back out into the exhibition.

They found Pavan and Flora's father, who were talking animatedly about a stand they had just passed that offered a newly invented "mobile phone". To Flora it just looked like a large telephone box with a bunch of wires sticking out of it.

"It only takes four men to carry it!" cried Pavan enthusiastically.

"Madness, it'll never catch on," said Flora's father.

Pavan ran over to her with a huge smile. "Dr Robinson asked me to join his dog-sled expedition to the North Pole!" he gushed excitedly. "He said he thinks my skills would be useful."

"Oh, that's wonderful!" said Flora. "What did you say?"

"I said I'd have to ask your father," said Pavan. "I wish you could come too – it wouldn't be nearly as much fun without you on the journey."

As they talked, they wandered past countless amazing, interesting and extremely odd stalls. People jostled each other to get closer to the stallholders so they could hear about their latest technologies.

"That's right, ladies and gentlemen, you heard me! I will reach the North Pole first!"

On hearing this loud, confident voice, Flora turned to see a man in a tall top hat at the next stall waving his cane excitedly in the air before pointing it at a huge poster of a ship.

"My ship, the *Endeavour*," he continued, "is an ice-breaker ship the likes of which no one has seen before! It is fitted with all the latest technology for slicing through the ice floes, including a reinforced hull and larger engines. With its extraordinary strength and speed, it will make short work of ice that has destroyed so many other boats. One at a time, one at a time, I beg you," he called to the crowd as they surged forward with interest. "I will answer all your questions!"

Pavan was already squeezing forward with the rest of the crowd, trying to take a closer look at the picture of the ship. Lavinia was hanging back, writing furiously in her notebook every time the man spoke.

"Can your ship really cut through ice?" Pavan asked the man with awe.

Dr Robinson's voice boomed out before the ship owner could answer. "Mr Crew's ship is just another shiny invention that's never been put to the test. My team will reach the North Pole first using *old* technology!"

The crowd round Mr Crew turned towards Dr Robinson, murmuring with interest.

"That's right," he said, his arms crossed with authority. "We'll use the same dog sleds that the Arctic peoples have been using for generations."

"Dr Robinson," asked a man with a notebook, "we've all heard of your plans to travel by dog sled, but do you really believe that your dogs will be faster than the *Endeavour*?"

Dr Robinson nodded confidently. "Absolutely. The dogs will allow us to travel over the ice in a direct route from Norway, whereas this shiny tin can has to take a longer route through much more dangerous waters."

He waved a dismissive hand at the poster of the *Endeavour*, provoking Mr Crew to shake his cane at him and shout, "I say, how dare you!"

"What about supplies? Will you be able to carry it all on sleds?" Flora asked, frowning. Surely those sleds couldn't carry enough food for the whole expedition, let alone having to also feed the dogs.

"We're well prepared, miss," he added. He gestured to Pavan, a smile cracking his stony face. "We'll be taking along plenty of this young lad's invention – the meal in a mouthful."

So many people seemed to have questions then, and they were all shouting over each other in a frenzy. But one voice carried above all the others, drawing everybody's attention. "I think you'll find there's a reason why the old ways haven't succeeded," called a handsome man with a moustache. "You might wish to see something new and daring instead!"

Mr Crew and Dr Robinson scowled at him.

Lavinia grabbed Flora's arm. "That's Mr Avery," she whispered. "The hot-air balloon pilot."

Flora took a good look at the balloonist. As he stood there with his hands on his hips and his eyes twinkling above a broad grin and a twirly moustache, Flora could imagine him as a dashing Robin Hood or pirate. He had an air of someone who goes on exciting adventures and who has a thousand stories to tell of daring escapes. The crowd seemed to have the same impression, as they all turned and were watching him with awed expressions.

"I'm sure you will agree, ladies and gentlemen, that the fastest way to travel is by balloon!" He dramatically swept his hand up and a huge curtain behind him dropped to reveal a magnificent hot-air balloon. There were gasps and one woman squealed with excitement.

"This beauty is but a smaller replica of the balloon I and my colleagues plan to use in our quest to reach the North Pole. There will be no concerns about hitting icebergs, nor will there be

fears about uneven landscapes or food shortages.
No! In comfort and, may I say, a great deal of
style, we shall sail straight to our goal and plant
our flag before anyone else has even had their
breakfast!"

Amazed applause rang out of the crowd. Mr
Avery grinned and took a bow.

"I pledge fifty pounds to your cause!" a man

shouted, raising his hand.

Flora and Pavan gasped, and Lavinia began writing in her notebook even faster. Fifty pounds was a lot of money!

Mr Avery nodded in gratitude. "Your help is appreciated, my good man!"

"I pledge seventy-five pounds! In cash!" A woman pushed through the crowd, her raised hand clutching several pound notes.

Mr Avery leant down and shook her hand before accepting the donation. Suddenly, the crowd surged, hands reaching forward to pledge money to help Mr Avery reach the North Pole in his balloon. Mr Avery seemed like an auctioneer, pointing and shouting joyfully, accepting the money that was thrust at him with real gratitude and a boyish grin.

"I pledge ONE. THOUSAND. POUNDS." A familiar voice boomed across the room. "If you let me join your crew." There was a pause, then an explosion of chatter as heads turned to see who offered such a vast amount of money.

"It's Lord Granville!" someone behind Flora shouted.

Flora gritted her teeth and glanced at Pavan, who rolled his eyes. Lord Granville was a heartless, greedy man who cared only for himself and his profits. When their paths had crossed in the hunt for the golden lotus, it was his exploitation of the rainforest that had almost killed them all. Thankfully, Flora had stopped him from destroying the golden lotus, but she was sure that he had never forgiven her for it! Flora shuddered to think that she had even been inside his house, which had a horrifying hall of animal heads. Lord Granville was bad through and through. He'd tricked society into thinking he was a philanthropist by donating money to good causes, but he always had an ulterior motive.

The crowd had turned and was now gathering round Lord Granville, who was smirking in the centre of it all. As always, he was sporting a pointed black moustache and beard, the finest clothes that money could buy, and a face that no right-minded person would trust. Meanwhile Mr Avery was bouncing on his heels, excitedly pointing at him.

"Lord Granville, what an honour!" he cried. "Please join me so that I can shake your hand!"

Lord Granville made his way through the throng of people. As he passed Flora and Pavan, however, he pushed them roughly out of his way and leant down to hiss, "You haven't won."

Without pausing to see their reaction, he walked straight past them and up to Mr Avery with a ready smile.

Flora turned away in disgust, unable to watch the scene. As she did, her eye was caught by a young girl around the same age as her, who was jumping up and waving her arm in the air, desperately trying to attract the attention of the explorers. She was well dressed in an expensive blue-silk dress, and her black hair was ornately done in the same style as Queen Victoria's, with plaits looped round her ears. The thing that drew Flora's attention the most, however, was the panic in her face.

To Flora's dismay the explorers ignored her, turning away and shaking their heads as if she were an annoying fly buzzing around them.

"Let's go, Nelly," said the girl's companion, a blonde woman in a governess's uniform.

Hanging her head in disappointment, the girl turned away. Flora noticed her eyes were brimming with tears.

She tugged at Pavan's arm, and together they approached the girl.

"Are you all right?" Flora asked.

The girl shook her head sadly. A tear slowly tracked down her face. "My parents had hoped to reach the North Pole too, but they went missing in the Arctic. I was hoping those men would help me find them."

"But they won't even give poor Nelly the time of day," said the governess indignantly.

"They refused to help?" cried Pavan in shock.

When Nelly nodded, Pavan made a disgusted noise, and Flora put a comforting hand on her arm.

"I'm so sorry to hear that," said Flora. "I'm Flora and this is my friend Pavan. We live nearby; why don't you come for a cup of tea and you can tell us about it?"

Nelly seemed to sag with relief and Flora wondered how long she had been at the exhibition, begging for help.

She smiled wearily at Flora. "Yes, please. I would like that very much."

# Chapter Three

They rounded up Flora's father and Lavinia, then walked from the Great Exhibition back to the house.

"Tell us everything," said Flora once Nelly was sitting comfortably in Flora's favourite chair.

"My father is Dr Norton, the Arctic explorer," said Nelly.

Her governess sat close by and leant over to

put a comforting hand on her arm. She looked extremely kind, with smiling blue eyes and curly blonde hair that refused to be tamed into a bun.

Behind them, Pavan used his latest invention to make them a cup of tea. It whistled and let out a puff of smoke, before perfectly brewed tea poured out of a spiralling copper pipe. The housekeeper Mrs Fairweather did not approve of this contraption one bit, and she scowled at it as she set down a tray of cakes on the coffee table.

Nelly and her governess gratefully accepted their cups of tea, and Pavan joined Flora, her father and Lavinia on the sofas to listen to Nelly's story.

"No one has heard from their ship for weeks, and it's been assumed that it was wrecked on one of the ice floes," she said.

"Your mother went to the Arctic too?" Mrs Fairweather blurted out in shock. "Surely that's no place for a woman!"

Flora stifled a laugh. Imagine how shocked Mrs Fairweather would be if she knew some of the adventures Flora had been on!

Nelly shook her head with a sad smile. "Yes, my mother is a famous singer, known as the London Lark. She was touring the concert halls of Scandinavia and joined my father on his expedition after her performances."

"Oh!" said Lavinia. "I heard your mother sing when she performed at the Royal Albert Hall. I wrote a glowing review in the newspaper."

"You must miss them very much," said Flora's father. Flora caught a flicker of sadness in his eyes and guessed he was thinking of her own mother. She wondered how many trips they had taken together, just like Nelly's parents.

Nelly nodded. "I'm certain they're still alive. Except no one will take me to the Arctic to find them, no matter how much money I offer! I even have a map that shows their route."

She unfolded a large map, which, after much shuffling of cake trays, was laid out on the coffee table. They all leant forward to see it.

"My mother performed in Denmark, Sweden and Norway before setting off for the North Pole," said Nelly, tracing the route with her finger.

"That's similar to the route I'll be taking with Dr Robinson's team," said Lavinia.

"You're sure you don't want to join the dashing Mr Avery's team?" teased Flora with a laugh, making Lavinia blush unexpectedly.

"Nonsense, there's only room for three on the balloon," she said, regaining her composure.

"Dr Robinson offered me a place on his team as well," said Pavan. "Perhaps he could find a place for Flora as well – she's good at finding things."

"I can probably persuade him that I need to

bring Flora so she can illustrate my newspaper article," said Lavinia.

So much was going on that Flora began to tic. It felt like the urgent feeling of needing to sneeze, but instead she started snorting like a pig. Which, of course, made her laugh, adding to the general chaos of the room.

"Calm down, everyone, calm down!" Flora's father had risen out of his seat and held his hands up, drawing everybody's attention. Silence finally settled among them.

"I don't think *anyone* should be going to the Arctic. It's too dangerous; so many boats have been wrecked there," he said, his voice kind and gentle as he turned to Nelly. "I'm so sorry. But the chances of finding your parents are very slim."

Nelly looked utterly heartbroken. Flora realised

that for a moment she must have felt the glow of hope. If Flora had ever had the tiniest glimmer of hope that her mother might still be alive, she knew how painful it would be to have that taken away.

She absent-mindedly touched the whale necklace that the spiritualist had given her.

As she did, she felt the carving send warmth into her chest. She paused, listening. Yes, she could once again hear that beautiful song, as sad as it was comforting. The notes seemed to move softly around her, growing in strength as she thought about Nelly's poor parents. She glanced around, but nobody else seemed to react to the music; it was as if only her ears could hear it.

The spiritualist's words echoed in her mind. *Follow the whale.*

"Please, Father. We need to go," Flora announced, full of conviction.

"*You're* not going anywhere, sir," said Mrs Fairweather, putting a firm hand on Flora's father's shoulder. "Your chest is still far too weak."

"I will keep an eye on Flora and Pavan, Mr Stormer," said Lavinia. "You have my word."

Flora looked at her father pleadingly, and then he nodded. "Fine."

"Will you really help me?" asked Nelly, her eyes shining with hope once more.

"Yes," said Flora, as her necklace sang. "We'll do everything we can to find your parents."

# Chapter Four

It was early in the morning when their boat drifted slowly into the port at Trondheim in Norway two weeks later. The sky was full of phantom mist, coloured pink and purple by the rising sun, while snow drifted down like they were in the middle of a gently shaken snow globe.

But the atmosphere in the port as they arrived was far from quiet. Crowds had gathered to welcome them with waving flags, their cheers loud and joyous. Flora and Pavan stood on the deck waving back at them with broad smiles.

"Nelly's parents' ship, the *Discovery*, was due to stop at Trondheim," Flora said, checking the map Nelly had given her as they walked down the gangplank and on to dry land.

"Well then, the first thing to check is whether they made it this far," said Lavinia confidently, reaching for her notebook. "Let's see what we can find out."

The land beneath their feet felt wobbly to Flora after being at sea – and combined with the ice that had formed along the town's streets, it felt like a recipe for a dramatic and very embarrassing fall. She gripped on to Pavan as they walked, who seemed equally unsteady, and they tried not to laugh when several crew members from their ship lost their balance. One man had given up trying to walk upright completely and was crawling along the high street on his hands and knees.

Lavinia didn't seem affected by the ice at all as she strode up to different groups of townspeople with a picture of the missing couple. Over and over again she was met with shaking heads, and it really seemed like their ship hadn't made it this far, let alone to the Arctic. *Poor Nelly,* thought Flora. How was she going to break the news to her?

"Let's take

a rest," Lavinia said after another unsuccessful interview.

"Good idea," said Flora, whose teeth were beginning to chatter. She was wearing her warmest jumpers and coat but somehow she still had goosebumps all over.

A cold wind whipped past them, making Flora tic. She had noticed that since arriving in the snowy climate, her tics had changed into ones that made her whole body shiver and tense up. Although it made her tired, as it used up a lot of energy, Flora was grateful to find that she felt a little warmer every time it happened.

"Over here!" called Pavan, standing at the entrance to a small café that glowed with a warm and welcoming light.

Soon they were settled into large squishy

armchairs beside a crackling fire while Lavinia went up to the counter to buy some food and drinks. Three cats, two black and white and one extremely fluffy ginger one, were curled up by the fire in a heap. It seemed like the cats had found the cosiest spot in Trondheim. As Flora warmed up, she noticed her normal tics were returning, and she bobbed her head up and down and scrunched her nose up.

Before long, the café owner placed three plates in front of them, each with a triangular slice of something that looked like a very flat cake.

"It's called lefse," said the café owner in answer to their questioning looks before walking away.

Flora took a bite and was delighted to find that it was filled with a cinnamon-flavoured buttercream that made her mouth water.

The café owner returned with two mugs of hot chocolate for Flora and Pavan, and a mug of something that smelt warm and spicy for Lavinia.

"What's that?" Pavan asked through a mouthful of lefse.

"It is glögg and not for children," said the café owner mildly but with a small warning look. "A sort of mulled wine with orange and spices."

Lavinia took a sip and melted into her armchair with a contented look. "Delicious!" she announced with a smile. "Oh, just a moment, please don't go," she said to the café owner as they began to drift away again. They paused.

"We're trying to find these people, Dr and Mrs Norton," said Lavinia, pulling out the picture and showing it to them. "Do you remember seeing them at all? We're trying to find out if they came through Trondheim."

The café owner took a long look at the picture. "Yes, they were here," they said with a nod.

"Really?" Flora cried a little too loudly, her excitement building.

"Yes," they said again. "I remember because I heard the lady sing. I will never forget the beautiful sound. They were different to the other adventurers that come through the town; they seemed very well prepared. I thought they had a real chance of reaching the North Pole."

After that unusually long speech, the owner turned and walked back to stand behind the counter.

Flora, Pavan and Lavinia all looked at each other, thinking the same thing. If Nelly's parents had made it to Trondheim and moved on towards the North Pole, then they would have to follow.

Lavinia got up to ask the owner where they might find the local guides, while Flora checked the map, stroking the whale necklace thoughtfully. Pavan stared longingly at the crackling fire, as if trying to absorb as much warmth as possible before they ventured out into the cold again.

The sky was lit by an eerie bluish daylight when they left the café, even though it was getting very late. All around them the town was brightly lit, with warm light spilling out of every door and window. It looked very welcoming, like a picture on a Christmas card, and Flora couldn't help but stop and sketch it for Lavinia's article.

Soon they reached a place where lots of people were gathering with their sleds. The men were tall and strong-looking. Each sled had six large and excited dogs attached to it, who were jumping and barking as if they were desperate to start running as soon as possible.

"These are the guides," said Lavinia as they approached. "There's no one better to guide us safely."

Dr Robinson, whose dog-sled expedition they were joining, was already there inspecting the different guides and dog-sled teams.

Flora's eyes were drawn to the only female guide. She was standing slightly to the side and surrounded by well-fed, happy-looking dogs. The dogs weren't tied to their sled like the others were, and instead were allowed to roam and play.

"Where did you get that amulet?" the woman asked softly as Flora approached.

Flora touched the whale necklace. "I was given it," she said.

The woman looked at it closely. She was wearing a thick animal-skin coat that almost reached the floor, while a fur hood surrounded her long plaited hair.

"It's a protective amulet, made here in the Arctic," she said. "See? I have one too."

She put her hand inside her coat and pulled out a necklace of her own. It was carved of wood, like Flora's, but was in the shape of a polar bear.

Flora compared the two amulets. How had

hers ended up in London in the hands of the spiritualist?

"What's your name?" Flora asked, bending down to stroke one of the dogs. The dog leant into her hand and closed its eyes happily. Behind her, another one of the woman's dogs gave an excited bark and jumped up at Pavan, so that its paws were on his shoulders and it licked his entire face.

"Kaya," the woman told her, smiling at them.

Flora touched the necklace, listening hard. Since they had arrived in the Arctic, the sound of the singing had been getting stronger, letting her know they were on the right path. But when she looked at Kaya, the singing became more powerful! It echoed around Flora, harmonising with itself and making the most beautiful song.

Flora knew what it meant.

*I'm following the whale, Mother. Just like you told me*, she thought.

Dr Robinson came over to Flora. "The guides have said they don't want the responsibility of children on their sleds."

Flora turned to her friends in dismay. Had they really come all this way only to fail?

Kaya stepped forward and put a hand on Flora's shoulder.

"I'll take her." She smiled at Pavan and Lavinia then added, "And her friends."

In the early hours of the next day, they stood on Trondheim's dock while the dog sleds were being loaded on to a ship. Excitement rippled through Dr Robinson's dog-sled team, and they chatted confidently about how they would win the race to the North Pole.

The excitement was infectious and Flora couldn't stop herself from smiling as she inspected Kaya's dog sled, which sat on the dock waiting to be loaded.

"I hope the dogs are fast. That sled won't do much to protect us if a polar bear catches us," she murmured thoughtfully.

Pavan yelped. "There are . . . POLAR BEARS?"

Flora looked up and grinned, clicking her tongue. The familiar urge made the back of her neck ache and she shook her head a few times.

"The Arctic is their natural habitat. So, yes, there are LOADS of polar bears." In the two weeks before setting off on their journey, she'd read every book she could find on Arctic wildlife.

"That's the least of our worries," said Lavinia, leaning close with a look of concern. "It's so cold there that we could get frostbite, which makes your fingers and toes go black and fall off."

Flora wriggled her fingers inside her new gloves that were lined with reindeer fur. On her feet she wore thick woollen socks inside the sturdy boots she'd bought for the expedition. She was grateful for her warm clothing, because over the two-day journey Flora was sure she could feel the temperature dropping every time she climbed on to the deck of the ship.

When they finally arrived in the icy Arctic, everybody stood on deck and looked around them in awe at their surroundings. Behind them was a soft backdrop of snow and fluffy clouds, welcoming and bright, while ahead of them was a dark and craggy landscape with a black sky. An ominous, icy wind rushed towards them as the dogs excitedly pulled on their harnesses, eager to disembark. Flora looked into that black sky and felt another rush of fear. Were they on a fool's mission? Maybe her father was right and Nelly's parents were already dead . . .

She was still feeling uneasy as they began to unload the dog sleds. It was impossible to turn back now, and nobody else seemed to be frightened. Soon the dog sleds were piled high with supplies, from tents to kayaks, and they were ready to set off. Flora was huddled into the bottom of Kaya's sled, while Lavinia took up the reins of another sled with Pavan at her feet. But before she could gather the courage to admit how she was feeling, the dogs began to run, taking them away from the safety of the ship and further into the wild.

As the sleds whizzed through the icy landscape, Flora turned the whale amulet over in her hands, listening to the comforting song. They were on the right path and it was urging her on.

The freezing wind whipped Flora's face until it felt like her skin was burning, and she pulled

her hood close round her. Her shivering tics were coming thick and fast, while every breath was searingly cold in her lungs; she wondered how anybody could survive here! All around them was a blank canvas of white snow and ice. The barking dogs and shouting men sounded odd and out of place, when everything seemed untouched by humans.

Through her snow goggles she looked about anxiously, searching for the thing she feared most. A tic surged up and before she could stop herself it leapt from her lips.

"POLAR BEAR!" she yelled.

Her hands flew to her mouth, but the damage was done! Everybody reacted, slowing the dogs sleds and shouting to each other as they raised their guns.

"Where is it?"

"Who saw a polar bear?"

"Protect the children!"

The only person who didn't show any panic was Kaya, who slowed their sled and scanned the white landscape with a confused expression.

"I'm so sorry," Flora called to the dog-sled team. "It was just a tic . . . I can't help it. There's no polar bear! Sometimes when I worry about something, I shout it out when I don't mean to."

Flora didn't know how else to explain her tics and was embarrassed that she'd caused so much chaos and panic. The men lowered their guns, shooting curious looks at Flora that made her want the ground to swallow her up.

Once the dog sleds were moving again, Flora looked determinedly ahead at the dogs bounding in front of her, desperate not to make eye contact with anybody. She was used to people being curious about her, and normally she didn't mind. But this time it felt like she had done something bad by causing all that panic, even if she hadn't meant to.

It wasn't long before a new distraction made her forget all about the polar bear tic.

"WHAT'S THAT?" one of the guides cried, their voice thin above the rushing wind.

Flora looked in the direction he was pointing to see something in the distance . . . Was that a boat? Yes, on the horizon she could see a huge ship tilting to one side and stuck in the ice. She felt a leap of excitement. Could it be Nelly's parents' ship, the *Discovery*? Had they finally found them?

# Chapter Five

They urged their dogs to go towards the ship, while Flora imagined the joyful reunion between Nelly and her parents. But as they got closer, Flora's excitement sank into disappointment. The ship wasn't the *Discovery*. It was the *Endeavour*! She recognised the ice-breaker from the poster she had seen at the Great Exhibition. It sat frozen ahead of them, eerily silent.

A sudden awful thought grew in her mind. She had heard of ships that had been found trapped in the ice in the Arctic, their only inhabitants the ghosts of their former crew. Ghost ships. The sight of the *Endeavour* frozen in the white ice made Flora shiver with fear. The words "ghost ship" echoed again and again in her head, until she had to say them out loud several times. Thankfully the tic was quiet and her words were lost in the rush of the wind.

"What are we stopping for?" cried Dr Robinson. "We must keep going!"

"But there might be people on board," said one of the guides.

"No, no, no!" Dr Robinson shook his head angrily. "The hot-air balloon is already ahead of us; we can't stop now if we want to get to the North Pole first! As leader of this expedition, I say we don't stop."

"No!" cried Flora. "We can't leave the people on that ship behind!"

"They'll die!" shouted Pavan.

"I'm sure they've already moved on," said Dr Robinson. "I only have one chance to get to the North Pole first, and I will not give it up for the sake of a pointless rescue mission."

He gestured at Lavinia. "Miss West, I assume

you're coming with us! We don't want you to miss my victory, do we?"

Lavinia frowned, looking from Dr Robinson to the *Endeavour*, and then at Flora and Pavan. After a moment of thought, she shook her head. "We have to help those people," she said, almost as if to herself rather than Dr Robinson.

Dr Robinson looked outraged but quickly composed himself. "Well, I can't force you to come with me," he grumbled. "I'm still expecting that article about my victory, and it had better be flattering."

He signalled to the guides and other members of his team, and with a shout to the dogs they moved off, leaving Flora, Pavan, Lavinia and Kaya behind. As they raced into the distance, the cold white landscape around them suddenly seemed very lonely and very dangerous.

"Did we make the right decision?" Pavan said nervously.

"It won't be hard to track them," said Kaya. She seemed to be the only one in the group who wasn't anxiously watching Dr Robinson's team as they sped further and further away.

"We made the right decision," declared Flora. She wrapped her coat more tightly round her as a shivering tic ran through her. "We have to help the people on that ship."

Lavinia nodded, still looking a little unsure. Flora knew she was wondering whether she ought to have stayed with Dr Robinson and covered the rest of the race for her article. She gave her friend a reassuring smile.

Without another word to each other, Kaya and

Lavinia hollered at the dogs and changed course, racing towards the ship. Flora turned round and watched Dr Robinson's team disappear from view. High in the sky, she spotted a colourful hot-air balloon, a distant dot on the horizon.

The ship loomed above them as they approached, and Flora breathed a sigh of relief as she saw the movement of people on the deck.

"Oh no!" cried Pavan from the bottom of Lavinia's sled.

Flora frowned, clicking her tongue several times. Wasn't it a good thing that the crew were alive? But as she peered closer, she too began to groan. There was a very familiar figure standing among them.

"SEE HERE, I paid good money to make sure I would get to the North Pole first! You said this ship was an ice-breaker, so . . . BREAK THE ICE!" The distant voice of Lord Granville was carried to them on the wind. He was waving his arms wildly at the captain.

"I *told* you," the captain said, a pained expression on his face. "The ship has its limits! We should have taken the safer route through the thin ice, like I planned, but you insisted we go through the thick ice because it was more direct."

*It was Granville's fault they were wrecked,* thought Flora as they came to a stop.

Looking up at the ship, Flora gasped in awe. Close up, it was an incredible sight. It looked so unnatural, a huge man-made object frozen at an odd tilting angle and surrounded by white ice and snow. How had it got there? There didn't seem to be any water for miles!

"Hello up there!" called Lavinia. "Do you need any help?"

The entire crew popped their heads over the side of the ship to greet them with joyous cries of relief.

"Oh, thank goodness!" called the captain.

"We were waiting to see if the icy conditions would improve so we could move the ship, but it looks like it's just getting worse. The ice is forming round the ship now. There's no way we can manoeuvre it out. We were too afraid to step on the ice in case it was thin and broke beneath us, but if you're down there it means it's safe."

A long rope ladder was flung overboard, and of course Lord Granville pushed everyone out of the way so he could descend first. He was wearing a coat made of thick bear fur, with the poor creature's head fashioned into a hood. On his feet were sealskin boots. Round his neck hung a muffler to keep his hands warm, which, to Flora's horror, looked like an entire stuffed Arctic fox. His twirly moustache looked like it was frozen solid, with long icicles hanging off it.

He gave Flora a disgusted look as he climbed on to the ice. "I'd heard you'd weaselled your way on to that dog-sled team. Always sticking your nose into other people's business, aren't you? I'm surprised you didn't force them to release the dogs into the wild," he said with a cruel sneer.

Clearly, he hadn't forgiven Flora for forcing him to close his rubber plantation on Isla Panacea on her last adventure.

Flora ignored him. She and the others began to help the rest of the crew climb down from the deck with vital supplies and skis.

"WHERE IS DANTE?" yelled Lord Granville suddenly. "I demand that you send him down to me at once!"

*Dante?* Flora was surprised that Lord Granville had brought his cherished pet ferret to such a cold and dangerous place. But then, she supposed, the two were inseparable. She had to stifle a giggle, however, when Dante was lowered from the deck – he was wearing a matching knitted coat and his whiskers had frozen into an icicle moustache that

perfectly matched
his owner's.

Lord Granville leapt
forward as Dante reached
the ground, snatching him
up and depositing him inside
his fox muffler so that only his little
white head and red eyes were visible, poking out
of one end.

"Will you be able to get back safely?" Lavinia
asked, frowning in concern.

The captain nodded. "Our guide has already
plotted the route, and we have enough skis and
supplies to make it to the ship rendezvous point."

"No, that simply won't do," said Lord
Granville, shaking his head angrily. "I want to win
this race. And I still can."

He strode up to Kaya. "You there. I demand you let me use one of your dog sleds."

Flora's eyes widened and she shook her head. Surely Kaya wouldn't agree . . .

As Lord Granville approached, he came close to the dogs who were harnessed to her sled. One of the dogs gave him a good sniff, then licked his gloved hand enthusiastically. Lord Granville leapt back with a disgusted noise, and Dante could be heard chattering in anger from within the muff. It looked as if it had taken all Lord Granville's willpower not to kick the dog.

Kaya had been watching closely with a little frown. After a pause, she simply shrugged and said, "OK."

Flora couldn't believe it. How had she ended up on another adventure with Lord Granville?

# Chapter Six

Long after they'd parted ways with the crew of the *Endeavour*, Kaya shouted over the rushing wind and barking dogs that they should stop and make camp.

"But it's still daylight," said Pavan, confused.

Kaya nodded. "This time of year we only get a few hours of darkness each day. It's still light but it's actually very late and we need to sleep."

They all worked together to build the tent, except Lord Granville who was relaxing on one of the sleds. He had a hand up the bottom of his stuffed fox muffler and was stroking Dante, who had his head sticking out of the mouth of the fox so that it looked as if it had eaten him.

This lazy behaviour was not new to Flora, who had frequently witnessed Lord Granville on Isla Panacea choosing his own comfort rather than helping others. Rather than getting cross, she turned away.

Soon Pavan was busy inspecting the sleds. He emptied his pockets on to the ice, until nuts, bolts and pieces of wire littered the ground round his feet, then he repaired any damage he found.

Kaya had just finished laying the fire and was throwing some preserved whale meat to the excited dogs. Flora watched curiously as Kaya then walked over to a hole in the ice a little way away from the camp. She turned and caught sight of Flora and with a smile gestured her to come closer.

As Flora approached, Kaya took some of the preserved whale meat and tossed it into the icy sea. They watched as it sank slowly down . . . down . . . into the darkness. How deep could the water be? Flora leant closer, staring as far into the depths as she could, when . . .

She gasped. In the darkness, swirling in the deep water, she noticed a soft green light. The light grew, rippling and gently spiralling until the sea was lit up with greens, blues and purples, as if the Northern Lights had risen from far beneath the ocean.

Flora gripped on to Kaya and leant further over the hole, mesmerised by the beautiful colours and movements, when she noticed figures dancing in the water below them. They looked like beautiful women, except . . . Flora stared, unable to believe what she was seeing. The figures had long glittering fish tails. Their fins swished in the water as they swam an intricate dance by the beautiful ocean light. Mermaids!

Flora leant nearer to the water's surface to get a better look. Suddenly, she felt her feet slip on the ice. She cried out and she fell forward. Luckily, Kaya managed to

catch her before she hit the freezing water.

"That was close," she said, righting herself with a grateful smile to Kaya. Her plaits, which had dipped into the water, were frozen solid already. Flora was sure that if any other part of her had fallen into the water, she would have been in serious trouble.

Kaya seemed to know what she was thinking. "Many people have died that way," she said with a nod. She peered down into the water as the figures disappeared. "The mermaids are like the Arctic. They are beautiful, but they are dangerous too . . ."

They sat

for a moment, both staring into the water as the lights faded away.

"You and I share something special," said Kaya, still watching the water. "We can both see things that others can't – the magic of nature. We are both different. Whoever gave you that amulet knew it too; they could see that special something inside you. A love of your fellow creatures."

Flora looked up at Kaya, and they smiled at each other.

The lights in the water had gone now, and so too had the dancing shadows. A thousand questions were bubbling in Flora's mind, and they began to spill out all at once.

"Were they really mermaids? Where do they come from? Have you ever met one?"

But Kaya only shook her head and gestured to

the tent. "Later. We must get out of the cold."

They looked over to see Lord Granville pushing past Pavan to enter the tent, loudly asking where the rest of them were going to sleep.

"Why did you let him join us?" Flora asked quietly.

There was a pause as Kaya thought this question over.

"It was the right thing to do. Just as I knew taking you and your friends was the right thing to do. Besides, I think it would be good for him. He does not respect nature, and perhaps after spending some time here, he will begin to appreciate it. Sometimes," she said, with a small frown, "sometimes the right thing to do is not the easiest thing."

It was smoky inside the tent, and a horrible

smell rose from the whale-blubber candles and curled into Flora's nostrils. But it was warm and oddly cosy. Outside, a howling wind whirled round the tent and Flora's skin prickled as the numbness from the day's cold slowly lifted. She had been ticcing all day, that shivering tic that went through her whole body, and she was starting to feel the exhaustion from it. She settled gratefully down on to a blanket beside Pavan and closed her eyes for a moment.

"What do we fancy for dinner tonight, fish, fish or fish?" Lavinia joked, handing out dried codfish.

Granville held up the fish and sneered at it. He showed it to his ferret Dante, who screeched angrily.

"This isn't food, it's torture! We had far better supplies on the ship. I made sure of that."

Flora thought she heard Lavinia grumble something about sending him back to the ship if he liked it so much.

"Kaya," Flora asked, "why did you throw that whale meat into the sea? Had it gone bad?"

The guide shook her head with a smile. "It was an offering for Velma, the sea goddess."

They all leant forward, the light of curiosity in their eyes. Even Lord Granville stopped scowling and was listening, stroking Dante who was curled on his lap.

Seeing their interest, Kaya put her fish down. In a low storytelling voice, she said, "Velma looks after all the sea animals, from the smallest baby seal to the mightiest narwhal, so my people always give her an offering to thank her for the meat from the animals we eat."

As Kaya spoke, Flora reached for her pencils
and began to sketch the guide.

"It's said that Velma possesses a mystical pearl
that can show you the future and the past. With
it, you can see any time and any place," Kaya
continued.

"We could look back and see what happened to
Nelly's parents!" Lavinia said with excitement.

"With the power to see into the future, you could make millions . . ." Lord Granville muttered to himself.

*I could see my mother again . . .* Flora thought back to the message she had received from her mother telling her to follow the whale. Maybe this was why she wanted Flora to come to the Arctic?

"Shame it's just a story," Pavan said.

But Kaya shook her head. "The pearl is as real as you or me. It's hidden in a mermaid lagoon east of here, near a lake that never freezes no matter how cold it gets. It's a magical and dangerous place. Few humans have ever been there.'

After seeing the swirling lights and dancing mermaids deep under the ice, Flora knew Kaya was telling the truth. She clasped the whale necklace tightly in her hands, listening as the singing grew louder and louder. It echoed around her head until it became deafening. Flora knew what she had to do. She had to go to that lagoon. She had to find the pearl!

# Chapter Seven

As the necklace's music died away, Flora heard a different noise – an odd scuffling sound outside the tent. And she wasn't the only one who could hear it. Unlike the whale's song, everyone could hear this rustling.

Flora gasped, jumping to her feet.

Kaya put a finger to her lips and reached for a large knife.

Lavinia mouthed what they were all thinking. *Polar bear.*

They all listened, frozen in fear, as the scuffling sound intensified. There was an ominous click as Lord Granville raised his gun and snapped off the safety catch, pointing it squarely at the tent entrance.

Suddenly, a jovial voice called out, "I say, is there room for three more?"

Pavan gave Flora a look as if to say, *A talking polar bear?* just as Mr Avery, the hot-air balloonist, poked his head into the tent and waved a bottle of champagne.

"We'll bring the bubbly if you don't mind sharing your dinner!"

There was an outburst of excited and welcoming chatter as they welcomed the three hot-air balloonists into the tent. Lord Granville lowered his gun with a calculating look on his face.

Soon they were all eating and chatting together, thawing out in the smoky warmth of the tent. Flora almost forgot the freezing landscape that waited outside.

"I don't understand," said Lavinia with a smile as Mr Avery topped up her mug with champagne. Flora had noticed that she had been smiling an awful lot since Mr Avery had appeared. "I thought you were ahead of us? We saw your balloon far off in the distance."

"Alas, the wind changed direction," he replied. "We blew so far off course that we decided to stop for a while. When we saw your tent, well, we couldn't resist some good company." He gave her a twinkling look.

"Now see here," said Lord Granville loudly, as if he was in the middle of a conversation with Mr Avery instead of barging into one.

Mr Avery looked up, startled. "What can I do for you, good sir?" he said, cheerfully ignoring Granville's rude behaviour.

"I'm going to join you on your balloon when you leave. You will take me to find this mermaid pearl I've been hearing all about. In return," he said, and waved a hand vaguely, "I don't know, I could guarantee you a knighthood. Would you like to be known as Sir Avery?"

Mr Avery laughed. "My dear chap, we'd love to give you a lift, but I'm afraid there's only room for three on the balloon."

"He's right," said Pavan enthusiastically. "It's down to physics. The balloon will have a maximum weight it can carry – any more than that and it won't lift off the ground."

With a look as cold as the ice around them, Lord Granville slowly lifted his gun and aimed it at Mr Avery's chest.

Everybody gasped and fell silent. Out of the corner of her eye, Flora saw Kaya silently pick up her knife. But Mr Avery shook his head at her, and said out loud, "It's all right, everybody, don't panic."

He looked at Granville calmly. Lord Granville

had a terrifying glint in his eye, one that Flora could remember seeing right before he tried to kill her on Isla Panacea.

"Perhaps I wasn't clear," snarled Lord Granville. "I'm taking that balloon. You and your crew will pilot it for me, or you can stay here to be eaten by polar bears."

Mr Avery looked over at his two crewmen, who both gave steely nods. His jaw clenched but he too nodded.

"You won't get away with this," cried Lavinia fiercely as Mr Avery and his two crewmen were marched out of the tent at gunpoint and into the harsh, windy tundra beyond.

They all rushed out of the tent, pale with horror, as they watched Lord Granville and his prisoners climb into the hot-air balloon basket.

"Oh, I think I will!" came Lord Granville's reply, carried thinly on the wind. "Once I get that pearl, I'll be the most powerful man in the world!"

With that, he yanked the tethering rope out of the icy ground and the balloon rose a little. Thanks to the weight of all four passengers, it hovered low in the sky.

With a frantic look in his eye, Lord Granville began throwing things over the side of the balloon to make it lighter. Equipment, food and fuel crashed to the ground below them, and in turn the balloon rose an inch or two higher.

Lord Granville looked down at the fox muffler hanging round his neck, and without another moment of thought he threw it, and Dante the ferret, overboard along with the rest of the discarded balloon contents.

It landed with a thump on the ice. Shakily, Dante the ferret crawled out from inside it, looking about in confusion. Lord Granville looked briefly down at the ferret before yelling, "Goodbye, losers!"

Flora watched with dismay as the balloon drifted eastwards in the direction of the mermaid lagoon. They couldn't let this happen. She turned quickly to rally the others into action, but it wasn't necessary. Pavan and Lavinia were already stowing away the tent, while Kaya was harnessing the dogs. They all knew what had to be done.

The race to the North Pole had become a race to the pearl.

# Chapter Eight

Flora's heart was pounding as they raced to catch up with the hot-air balloon. It hovered low ahead of them, its ropes trailing behind it, but it always seemed just out of reach no matter how fast the dogs ran.

There was a crash as something hit the ice in front of them, and Kaya had to sharply swerve to avoid a box of food rations. There was another crash, and then another and another as coiled rope, sandbags and navigational instruments showered from the sky. High up in the balloon, Lord Granville had started throwing things overboard again in an attempt to gain more height. Flora had a twisting feeling in her stomach as, to Granville's delight, the balloon finally began to rise and move faster.

Soon the balloon had disappeared into the distance and the sleds had been left behind.

"What do we do now?" Pavan cried.

"We keep going," Flora shouted, determination steeling her voice.

After a few hours, Kaya called for the sleds to stop. When Flora asked what was wrong, Kaya frowned and pointed. "Look," she said.

Flora followed her gaze to see something

. . . pink? Here and there in the snow were pink patches, which formed a trail leading to a crumpled shape ahead of them. *Oh no . . .*

Kaya spoke, confirming their worst fears. "It's blood . . ."

Flora looked away, too frightened to find out which of the crew had been thrown overboard so that Lord Granville could get to the pearl first.

"Stay here, I'll go and look," said Kaya, grimacing.

"I'll go with you," Lavinia said. She turned to Pavan and Flora with a fiery look in her eye. "You two wait here – do not follow us."

They watched as Lavinia and Kaya, bent into the freezing wind, slowly approached the figure. Flora looked over to Pavan huddled in the bottom of the other sled, who seemed just as frightened as she was. Even Dante, who they had taken with them in Flora's sled, poked his head out of the fox muffler to watch.

Soon Lavinia and Kaya were making their way back to the sleds with grim expressions on their faces.

"Well, it's not a member of the balloon crew," she said.

Flora frowned. Wasn't that a good thing? Why did they both look so upset then?

"It's . . ." Kaya began, but she seemed too appalled to say it.

"It's a polar bear," said Lavinia quickly with a grimace. "He's killed a polar bear."

"How do you know it was Lord Granville?" asked Pavan weakly.

"He took its head," said Lavinia simply.

"Why? Why would he do that?" Kaya burst out. "There's no respect in it. When an animal is hunted, every part of it should be used for the good of all. It should be thanked and honoured, not thrown away as if its sacrifice was worth nothing."

Kaya was extremely upset and was staring wildly about her as if the world had stopped making sense to her. Her dogs, who seemed to sense her distress, started howling and moving restlessly.

"I know why," said Pavan quietly. "He collects animal heads."

Flora thought back to the horrifying wall of stuffed animal heads she'd seen the one time she had visited Lord Granville's mansion, back when Pavan was still his apprentice. In her memory she could clearly see an empty plaque engraved with "Polar Bear". The poor creature was just another collectable item to Lord Granville. She ticced the word "polar bear" and scrunched her nose up, but in the cold temperatures it didn't make the aching feeling go away until she had done a full-body shiver.

"We have to honour it." Kaya's words were a statement, not a request.

They all immediately agreed. They may have been in a race to reach the pearl first, but this was important. Flora felt as if she were constantly trying to undo the damage that Lord Granville was wreaking upon the world.

"Lavinia and I will take what we can from the polar bear. Will you two give this offering to Velma?" Kaya handed Flora a small parcel, which she knew contained a piece of the polar bear. Flora was very grateful that Kaya had wrapped it up for her.

"You go," said Pavan to Flora. "I'm going to see if I can make a smaller towing sled out of the things Lord Granville threw overboard, so we have more space for storage."

As they all walked in different directions, Kaya's voice was carried to Flora on the wind.

"It's all my fault," she said sadly to Lavinia. "I should never have brought him from the ship. I should never have told you people about the pearl."

"We're not all like him," said Lavinia.

Flora looked over her shoulder to see Lavinia put an arm round Kaya as they walked off towards the bear's form.

Feeling desperately sad, Flora knelt at a hole she had found in the ice. She opened the parcel that Kaya had given her and dropped the offering into the water. As she watched it sink gracefully down into the dark waters below, she whispered a message that she hoped Velma would receive.

"Please don't let Lord Granville get the pearl. He's a bad man who has done terrible things, and if he gets the pearl, no one will be able to stop him. Please help us."

As she finished speaking, the soft bluish light that she

had seen before lit up the water, making it look as if the Northern Lights were dancing in its depths. Remembering Kaya's warning about keeping away from the water's edge, Flora had to resist the urge to creep closer to see if she could catch a glimpse of the mermaids.

She desperately wanted to see a mermaid close up. *Can they speak?* she wondered. *Do they have gills?* But she had to content herself with watching shadowy figures flitting about in the water far beneath her, and felt lucky that she had been able to witness that much.

As they prepared to set off again, Flora noticed Kaya crouched in front of the sled. Kaya was holding up a piece of meat, trying to tempt Dante out of the fox muffler. Every now and then his little head popped out and he tried to snap at her fingers, but Kaya continued trying to coax him out.

"I wouldn't bother," said Pavan, walking over. "That ferret is the meanest creature I've ever met."

"He's just missing his owner. He's scared and confused," said Kaya.

Pavan gave Flora a look that said *Why would anyone miss Lord Granville?* before wandering off towards his and Lavinia's sled.

"Is everyone ready? We'll have to work hard to catch them up, but I think it's still possible," said Lavinia.

"There is a short cut . . ." said Kaya hesitantly. "It's quite dangerous, though."

Out of nowhere, the whale amulet round Flora's neck began to grow warm. She touched it curiously and felt the soft hum of magic running through it. She could hear the whale's song but it sounded oddly shrill and shrieking in a way that put Flora's teeth on edge and made her tongue ache with the need to tic. She clicked her tongue, but while the shrieking continued the ticcing feeling would not go away.

Kaya pointed at an ice formation to their left. "That's a glacier," she said. "There's a crack that runs all the way through it, just wide enough for our sleds. But the ice in a glacier can move over time so there's no way of knowing whether the crack still runs all the way through to the other side."

Lavinia frowned, calculating. "How much longer will it take if we take the safe route?"

"Days," Kaya said with a grimace.

"That means if we take the short cut, we might

just get to the pearl before Lord Granville," said Pavan, excitement making him bounce.

Flora thought about Nelly's parents, who could be out there in the Arctic, running low on supplies. The mystic pearl was their best shot at finding them. There was no time to lose.

"That settles it then," Flora declared. "Let's take the short cut."

They all nodded, their mouths set with determination. As they turned and made their way towards the glacier, Flora closed her eyes and held the whale necklace. The mystical song was growing more beautiful with every moment. They were moving in the right direction!

The ice formation loomed high above them as they approached it at full speed. It was so much larger than she had realised: a wall of bluish ice that went on for miles in both directions, so tall that she had to crane her neck to see the sky above it. And there was the crack in the ice wall that Kaya had seen. It was a dark line from the base of the formation all the way to the top, as jagged as a broken bone. It looked pencil thin at first, but as they approached it grew wider with every second. It didn't look inviting. It looked very, very dangerous.

Flora wanted to slow down and approach the crack in the ice wall cautiously, but Kaya called for the dogs to go faster.

"We must go as fast as we can," shouted Kaya to Lavinia. "Cracks in the ice are very unstable. Ice or rocks could fall on us, or, worse, our presence could cause an avalanche. We need to get out the other side as quickly as possible."

Kaya's words planted a seed of fear in Flora's
heart, and she closed her eyes tight as they
approached the opening in the ice.

Suddenly, even though her eyes were closed,
she knew they were inside the ice formation. The
frozen wind had dropped and instead she felt
the cold breath of the ice walls as they closed in
round her. Nervously peeping out from her thick

hood, she noticed that the light had changed so that everything was tinted a shadowy blue. She was expecting the ice walls to be covered in jagged shards but instead found that they were smooth.

The dogs were yapping to each other nervously as they ran, and the noise echoed around them in a very unnerving way. Soon the light bled away as they sped deeper and deeper into the ice. All Flora could do was stare upwards at the tiny sliver of sky she could still see and trust that the dogs would keep them safe. As the darkness descended, the dogs fell quiet. The only sounds Flora could hear were of running paws and the ominous creaking of the ice. In front of her, Dante started making frightened little chattering noises. Unnerved, Flora had a growing feeling that told her to scrunch her nose up over and over. No matter how many times she did it, however, the feeling just wouldn't go away.

"Look!" cried Pavan from somewhere in the darkness ahead of her.

"I see it! We're nearly there!" replied Lavinia.

Ahead of them, a tiny sliver of white light glowed in the darkness. They had reached the other side!

"Something's wrong," called Kaya.

Flora didn't know whether it was the words she had said or the fear in her voice that was more terrifying.

"The walls are closing in. I don't know if the exit will be wide enough for us to get through!"

The opening in the ice was getting closer now, and the darkness ebbed into that extraordinary bluish light again. Flora could see exactly what

Kaya meant. The walls of ice were close. There was no more than an arm's length between each side of the ice, and the gap was getting narrower and narrower. There was no way they would be able to squeeze through the last part of the tunnel!

"Pavan!" yelled Flora. "Pavan, is there anything on your sled that you can use to tilt it on to its side?"

"Not if we don't want the dogs to get hurt!" cried Pavan. "What should we do?"

Fear had frozen Flora's mind. All she could think about was the awful crash they were moments away from having. Lavinia and Kaya both tried to slow down before the sleds were broken apart, but the poor dogs were running too fast to slow down in time.

Flora frantically clutched the whale necklace

in her hands, listening to the serene song that came from it. It grew louder and louder until Flora had to let go of it so that she could cover her ears. Still the high-pitched notes grew in volume, echoing around the ice until Flora noticed cracks forming in the walls!

"The ice beneath us is splitting!" cried Kaya.

Only Flora knew that it was the whale's song causing the ice around them to fracture, because only she could hear its deafening music. Was it angry that they had taken the wrong route?

Without warning, the ice beneath Lavinia and Pavan's sled cracked and they dropped out of sight.

# Chapter Nine

"Hold on to something!" yelled Kaya.

Her stomach filled with dread, Flora gripped on to the sled and screamed as they plunged through the same hole in the icy floor that her friends had just disappeared into. But instead of falling to an awful doom, they landed in a tube-like slide made entirely out of ice.

"WOOHOO!" came Pavan's whoops of joy

from somewhere further down the tunnel.

The dogs in front of Kaya and Flora's sled were all on their bellies, legs splayed and tails wagging, as they slid through the icy tunnels, spiralling round bends and soaring across chasms. It was incredible! Flora couldn't believe that moments ago she had expected a catastrophic crash, and instead they were sliding through beautiful icy passageways!

The light was somehow brighter down there and the ice seemed alive with those same blues, greens and purples that Flora had seen deep in the water whenever an offering had been made to Velma. Every now and then Flora was certain she caught sight of a fluttering fishy tail inside the ice, but the sled was moving far too fast for her to know for certain whether she'd seen a mermaid.

Behind them was a panicked squeak. Flora turned to see Dante bouncing and sliding along the icy tunnel. He must have fallen out of the sled when they fell! Kaya reached back to try to grab him, but with an alarmed look in his eye he slid straight past the sled, twisting and turning on the ice until he was within teeth-snapping distance of the dogs. Realising this, he made little swimming motions with his tiny arms, trying to get further away from them, until with another echoing squeak he disappeared into a small hole in the ice beneath them.

Flora gasped and scrambled forward. Was he gone?

But no – she could see a small figure zooming through another tunnel below, warped and magnified through the sheet of ice between them.

She watched as Dante whizzed along, looped over and above them, then flew out of an opening in the wall. He soared through the air, eyes bulging in fear, straight into Kaya's waiting arms.

Finally, after laughing and whooping their way through the magical tunnel system, the icy walls opened out into daylight, and they came to a sliding stop on a flat patch of icy ground.

"That was . . . unexpected," said Kaya as she climbed off the back of the sled. Dante was trembling inside her hood, gripping on to her plaits with a haunted look on his face.

"That was amazing!" shouted Pavan, arms raised into the air.

Lavinia, who had already pulled out her notebook and was struggling to hold her pen with her big mittens on, laughed. "That was front-page worthy!" Clumsily, she started jotting down notes.

Flora took a deep, steadying breath and looked about her. In front of the sleds was a huge body of water, fragments of ice floating on its surface. Behind them, far in the distance, she could see the glacier that had almost claimed their lives. Had Velma helped them on their journey?

Flora bobbed her head up and down, and then did it again, as she scanned the horizon for the hot-air balloon. She couldn't see it anywhere. Were they already too late? Her stomach twisted nervously. "We have to catch up with Lord Granville and stop him from reaching the pearl first!" she said, suddenly full of panic.

"You're right, but we can't go by sled from here," said Kaya, shaking her head.

She gestured to the dogs, who were all sniffing

the air and pacing. Some of them lay down and covered their faces with their paws, while a few of them began to howl.

"There's something in the air they don't like. They're frightened. I don't want to make them go any further; it's not fair on them."

Flora couldn't smell anything except the frozen air that burnt her nose. But when she concentrated, she felt a strange humming that made the hair on her arms stand up. Could the dogs be sensing the magic of the mermaid lagoon?

"We'll make a camp here for the dogs and leave them to rest while we finish the journey by kayak," said Kaya, unhooking the kayaks from the sleds before tending to the dogs.

"I'll stay at the camp with the dogs," said Lavinia. "The poor things shouldn't be left alone."

Kaya frowned. "I don't want anyone to be at the camp by themselves; it's too dangerous."

"I'll stay too," said Pavan confidently.

"But . . ." Flora didn't know how to tell them that she was afraid of going on without them. Then she closed her mouth, knowing that if her friends were brave enough to stay at the camp on their own, she could be courageous enough to continue the journey to the lagoon without them. She thought about Nelly back in London, missing her parents. Flora needed to be brave for her.

"Good luck!" said Pavan.

"Stay safe," said Lavinia, giving Flora a hug.

Soon they were pushing off the ice and floating out into the water, leaving the animals, Lavinia and Pavan behind.

The kayaks were long and very thin, with space

for only one person each. Kaya had told them they were made from driftwood and waterproofed animal skins, which of course Pavan had found fascinating. Flora wouldn't have been surprised if she caught him making one of his own when they got home to London! But now that she was sitting in one, floating out among the shards of ice in the dark, freezing water, she wasn't sure she liked the experience very much. And she was having trouble steering.

"Paddle left to go right, and right to go left," called Kaya over her shoulder. "Don't worry – a kayak is very stable."

As Kaya paddled ahead of her, Flora peered into the water nervously. It was so deep that it was almost black. Flora shuddered at the thought of all the creatures swimming far below her. The

thought made her click her tongue and bob her head up and down, and she pushed away the need to shout "polar bear!".

Flora dipped her paddle in the water, switching from side to side. She was starting to get the hang of the technique. The water lapped at the sides of her kayak as she looked back at the shore, which seemed far away. Had they really paddled such a distance? She felt like a tiny speck floating out into danger.

All of a sudden, the water began to bubble up around her in a frenzy of motion.

"Help!" she cried.

But Kaya was struggling too, as water frothed round her kayak. "Hold tight!" she urged Flora.

Huge fins splashed in the water and hit Flora's boat, almost toppling her out, when the water became eerily still. Flora righted herself in her kayak, then looked about her and gasped. One by one, creatures were rising out of the water, fierce expressions on their faces as they surrounded the kayaks.

Mermaids!

# Chapter Ten

The mermaids said nothing at all as they took hold of the kayaks and pulled them through the water. Flora and Kaya were utterly helpless and sat with their paddles on their laps, waiting to see what the mermaids would do with them.

They certainly did not look friendly. They were similar to the ones in the storybooks Flora's father had read to her, only much more frightening.

They wore fierce, scowling expressions beneath frosty white hair and eyebrows.

It was eerily quiet. The only sounds were the lapping of the water, the heavy beating of Flora's heart, and the soft thump, thump, thumping of the mermaids' tails as they beat against the bottom of her boat as they pulled her along.

As they silently guided the kayaks through

the water, Flora wondered if the bluish tint to their skin was because of the icy cold water they swam in. She had to quickly look away, however, because the pearlescent scaly patterns on their tails were starting to make her need to tic.

Even though Kaya was nearby, Flora felt alone and very vulnerable in her small kayak. The mermaids were so close that she could touch them, which of course meant that they could touch her if they wanted to. Were these really the beautiful figures she had seen dancing deep underwater?

Soon they were pulled into the wide dark entrance of an icy cave. Flora winced as her boat drifted under countless menacingly sharp icicles that hung from the ceiling, dripping so often into the water that it looked as if it was raining inside the cave. Once or twice a freezing droplet of water hit her face or went down the back of her coat, making her scream before she could stop herself.

A few of the mermaids turned to look at her with narrowed eyes. One even bared her teeth.

The whole situation felt far too menacing. A shiver ran down her spine and she shook her head so violently that she saw stars.

"Kaya," she whispered as their kayaks drifted closer together. Her voice echoed around the cave. "Do you think they're going to hurt us?"

"Nobody will be hurt as long as we're respectful," Kaya whispered.

Another worrying thought popped into Flora's mind – what if Nelly's parents had encountered the mermaids and something had gone wrong?

Dante's head appeared at Kaya's shoulder. He

looked about them, noticed the mermaids and gave a terrified squeak before diving once more into Kaya's cosy reindeer-skin coat. She patted the Dante-shaped bulge reassuringly.

Trying to calm herself, Flora pictured Pavan and Lavinia back at the camp. What would they think of these beautiful, frightening creatures? Well, Pavan would probably tell them to eat Dante first so they'd have some time to escape, she thought with a smile.

"Can you feel the magic in the air? They're taking us to the mermaid lagoon," said Kaya with hushed awe.

Yes, Flora could feel the magic. She had goosebumps and this time it wasn't because of the cold! There was an electric, crackly feeling all around them, as if anything could happen, and it was getting stronger as the mermaids pulled the kayaks through the cave.

Softly, the whale necklace round Flora's neck began to sing. The sound echoed off the icy walls, overlapping with itself in a beautiful harmony that calmed Flora. It was such a shame that nobody else could hear it, she thought. As she touched the necklace, it began to grow warm against her chest. It was like having the protective arms of a guardian round her.

"What's that noise?" asked Kaya suddenly.

Flora frowned, wondering if Kaya could hear the music too, but the guide had turned round in her kayak to look behind them. Flora turned as well, just in time to hear a crack and then a splash. And then another. And another.

When she realised what was happening, her

eyes widened in horror. "The icicles are falling into the water!" she cried.

"We have to get out of here fast."

Kaya tried to dip her paddle back into the water, but the mermaid who held her boat turned round and hissed angrily.

"There's nothing we can do," Kaya said, looking up at the icicles above them with real fear. "We're in their hands now."

It wasn't just the icicles behind them that were breaking off now. All around them sharp shards of ice were breaking off from the ceiling and plunging into the water, making it churn and rock their boats.

Flora leant close to the mermaid who was guiding her boat. "Please! Please can you hurry? We need to get out of here!"

But the mermaid just frowned and kept moving at the same slow pace.

Finally, there came the most terrifying splintering and groaning noise from above their heads. Flora looked up. Above them was a huge icicle that looked as deadly as a sharpened arrow, and it was creaking and cracking as if it was ready to break off the icy ceiling and plunge straight into their boats. They held their breath as they floated slowly beneath it. Flora was sure it was going to fall on them. Why weren't the mermaids speeding up to avoid it?

The moment their kayaks were out from under it, the massive icicle fell with a thundering

crash, showering them with freezing droplets and
making the water churn and swell, until . . .

"Watch out, it's a tidal wave!" Flora cried.

The wave picked up the kayaks and carried
them on foaming white water that threw them
around violently as it rushed through the icy
caves. It was all Flora could do to cling to her
kayak until the wave pushed them out of the ice

caves and into a calm body of water. As quickly as the wave had appeared, it dispersed, leaving her blinking in the blinding sunlight and wondering where she was.

Once her eyes adjusted to the bright light, Flora peered around. To her relief Kaya was there too, looking just as stunned. They were floating inside a large ring-shaped iceberg, with a lagoon of water in the middle of it. White and bluish ice rose high above them on every side, and Flora could barely see the patch of pale blue sky above them.

She stared about in wonder, until she finally turned her head and locked eyes with a woman who was sitting on an impressive throne flanked by two enormous polar bears, wearing collars made from seashells.

Flora gasped in disbelief.

The woman sat before them was giant in stature and was certainly as large as the polar bears beside her, with wild hair that moved like seaweed in the ebb and flow of the tides. She stared at them with a commanding, expectant expression. There was no doubt in Flora's mind that this was Velma.

"What do you want from me?" she demanded, her voice echoing.

"We're trying to find a friend's lost parents," Flora said, trying to sound confident. "Your pearl . . . well, we think it would help us find them."

"And you would have me give it to you? Just like that?" said Velma angrily.

The water around them rippled as the mermaids who had escorted Flora and Kaya to the lagoon swam towards Velma. They climbed out of the water and sat round her, making soothing noises and combing her hair with coral brushes. The frown that had thundered across Velma's brow began to soften. *They're calming her*, Flora realised with surprise.

"We just wanted to borrow it," explained Flora. "To see what happened to my friend's parents. Please will you help us?"

Velma gave a meaningful look to one of the mermaids. The mermaid nodded, then dived back into the water. When she surfaced, she reverently held a huge shell above her head and, with a bow, passed it to Velma. Inside the gigantic scallop shell was the biggest pearl Flora had ever seen

The pearl was magnificent. It was far larger than Flora had expected, about the size of a football, and gleamed an iridescent peachy colour.

She recognised it instantly. It was the crystal ball she had been shown by the spiritualist at the exhibition!

She frowned, staring at Velma. Yes . . . she could see traces of the spiritualist's features in Velma's face, and the goddess was also missing one of her hands. Her eyes flashed with a purple

shimmer. Had Velma been the spiritualist who gave her the whale necklace? Flora touched the necklace softly and it grew warm against her chest.

Velma waved her hand so that images began to appear on the surface of the pearl, just like she had at the exhibition. The first picture that appeared was of a young girl being hugged by her father.

"I had a family once too," said Velma sadly.

The mermaids continued to comb her hair and sing in her ear. While Velma talked, the water around Kaya and Flora was disturbed as sea animals began to rise out of it. A huge walrus, white tusked and leathery-skinned, heaved itself on to the ice. A group of seals popped their heads out of the water around the kayaks. The polar bears lay down, their muzzles nestled on their paws. All were watching Velma and all were listening to her story.

"When I refused to marry who my father wanted, he threw me out of my kayak."

The image changed to show the girl, older now, being thrown from her kayak by the man. Flora gasped. The man looked so calm when he did it, it frightened her. She thought about her own kind and loving father, and felt so sad for Velma.

"I tried to cling to the side of the kayak. I tried to climb back in," continued the goddess. "But he chopped off my fingers and then the rest of my hand to prevent it."

"No . . ." whispered Flora in agonised shock. She closed her eyes so she wouldn't have to watch that part of the story on the pearl's surface.

"Yes," Velma said, her voice like steel. "I

watched as my fingers sank into the dark waters.
As they did, they transformed into sea animals
and I into the goddess of the sea."

Flora peered back at the magical images Velma
was conjuring just in time to see the young
woman sinking deep into the ocean, with whales
and seals and walruses spiralling around her.
When the woman reached the ocean floor, she

curled up in a ball of sadness. Velma watched the image for a moment, frowning at the memory.

"My father rejected me because I was different. My sadness overwhelmed me and I cried many, many tears. Those tears froze into a pearl. They formed the pearl that you seek."

The images dispersed and silence settled on the lagoon as they all thought about what they had seen. How many tears had Velma shed to create such a huge pearl?

"I'm so sorry such an awful thing happened to you," whispered Flora with emotion. "I'm different too. I know what that's like . . ." She looked at Kaya and gave her a small smile. "But I've been lucky enough to find friends who accept me as I am."

She glanced back at Velma, unsure how the

goddess would react. Velma stared at her intently for a long time. Flora began to feel self-conscious. She jerked her head up twice and clicked her fingers several times, but Velma did not react to the tics. Suddenly, she turned to one of the mermaids combing her hair.

The mermaid took the pearl from its shell then dived into the water, emerging beside Flora's kayak. Her head bowed, she held the pearl up to Flora.

But then a shadow swept across the lagoon. They all looked up in confusion, just as the hot-air balloon drifted across the sky, blocking out the sun. Lord Granville appeared at the edge of the balloon's basket and it began to slowly descend.

"You!" he yelled, pointing at Flora. "Give me that pearl!"

# Chapter Eleven

On hearing his master, Dante wriggled out of Kaya's coat and scurried to the end of her boat so that he could stand on his hind legs and squeak up at Granville. *That little traitor*, thought Flora, narrowing her eyes at the ferret.

"And give me back my pet!" cried Granville when he saw Dante, in more of a whining tone.

It appeared that Lord Granville couldn't see

Velma or her mermaids. Flora wondered if Velma's magic was like that of the rainforest spirits on Isla Panacea; only those with a true affinity to nature could see and sense its magic.

Velma could see Lord Granville, though. She looked at him with a cold glare, as if she had just spotted an irritating fly buzzing around her head.

But Lord Granville was far more dangerous than a fly. He aimed his gun straight at Flora.

"No!" cried Flora in horror.

As Granville fired the gun, Mr Avery

appeared behind him and pulled him away from the basket's edge, so that the bullet ricocheted off the end of Flora's kayak and disappeared into the water.

"HOW DARE YOU!" thundered Velma, standing up to her full height. Her voice echoed with outrage around the lagoon, cracking the ice and making the sea churn.

Flora desperately held on to her kayak, trying not to capsize and fall into the water.

Velma's eyes flashed with fury as she stood with her arms raised, whirling a violent sea storm into being. The skies grew dark with grey and purple clouds that threw down sheets of rain and flashed with forks of lightning. The once still waters of the lagoon frothed with waves that had appeared out of nowhere.

"You have tricked me," cried Velma, pointing an accusing finger at Flora.

"You don't understand!" sobbed Flora. "That man is against us, not with us!"

"Do not try to manipulate me any more! You have taken advantage of me and I will make you all pay. ATTACK THE INTRUDERS!"

At these words the animals that had been listening to Velma's story dived back into the water. The mermaids screeched, baring their sharp teeth, and followed. Soon Flora and Kaya weren't just battling the raging waters, they were also trying to survive the attacks of the animals and the hands of the mermaids who were trying to pull them overboard.

High above them, the hot-air balloon was being tossed about in the stormy skies. With a great crash, it hit one of the walls of ice that surrounded the lagoon and started to drift downwards. With an athletic leap Mr Avery jumped out of the balloon and into the water just before it hit the icy ground with a sickening crunch.

Flora was fighting for her life. She felt the mermaids' cold, slimy hands grabbing at her. Suddenly, a huge spear-like horn rose out of the water. A narwhal! The huge grey creature pointed its long horn directly at her and swam towards her boat.

There was nothing she could do. The narwhal charged, tossing her kayak and plunging Flora into the icy water.

She surfaced with a spluttering gasp and looked around with wild panic. The water was so cold she could barely draw a breath. "Kaya? Where are you?" she cried.

Had her friend survived? Among the chaos, she spotted Kaya pulling Mr Avery on to her boat from the water, out of the mermaids' grasp. As soon as he was on board, Mr Avery grabbed the paddle and began fighting off a walrus that was trying to capsize them. But they hadn't yet spotted the polar bear that was determinedly swimming towards them!

"Look out!" shouted Flora.

Dante appeared at Kaya's shoulder, barking aggressively before launching himself at the polar bear's head.

Flora knew she had to get out of the water. It was so cold that her entire body was trembling, and she was beginning to lose the feeling in her fingers and toes. If she stayed there any longer, her whole body would seize up and she would sink like a stone.

She started to swim towards Velma. Maybe she could talk to her, explain that they hadn't tricked her? But as she swam towards the ice at Velma's feet, their gaze met. The goddess's eyes were full of fury.

Flora's attention was pulled away from Velma, however, as she noticed Dante splashing about in the water to her right. He was squeaking and struggling against the stormy waves, desperately trying to keep his little head above the surface. Flora immediately changed course and began to swim towards Dante. As she reached him, he gratefully climbed straight into her arms.

Suddenly, a pair of icy-cold hands grabbed Flora's feet and dragged her under the water's surface.

When the mermaid finally let go of her, Flora, still holding Dante, was deep underwater. Desperately holding her breath, she looked up to see that the surface was too far away to reach. It shimmered and churned with movement, but everything around Flora was still in the half-darkness of the deep ocean. Mermaids surrounded her, fierce and frightening, waiting for her to drown.

Flora's lungs ached, and the cold water was numbing her entire body. Dante looked up at her sadly, his eyes softly closing. She knew he

wouldn't last much longer. Even though her
muscles screamed with the effort, she launched
him upwards through the water, and watched
as he rose to the surface. It had used up her last
strength, and she knew she would not be able to
save herself as well.

As Dante's head broke the surface of the

water, the whale amulet round Flora's neck sent a powerful pulse out into the water, scattering the mermaids in every direction. But it was too late for Flora to swim to the surface now. She closed her eyes, listening as its magical singing filled the water.

It was the most lovely, angelic sound Flora had ever heard.

# Chapter Twelve

A large hand plunged through the water. It grasped Flora's coat and with great force she was pulled upwards and out of the frigid lagoon.

The air was sharp and painful in Flora's lungs but she was grateful for it. She lay on the ice, coughing and spluttering, until she was finally able to breathe easily again. Shivering, she sat up and looked about her in confusion. Now she was soaking wet. Cold wind whipped past her neck, making it ache with the urge to tic. But she was trembling so much that she wasn't even sure if it was her tics or the freezing temperatures that were making her shake.

Velma was standing with her back to Flora, her arms raised but this time in a calming manner. The sky was clearing and the wind dying away. The goddess spoke softly to the animals, who stopped attacking Flora and her friends.

Finally, Velma turned to Flora. She lay a huge hand on Flora's chest, and it immediately felt as if Flora were sitting beside a warm, crackling fire. She felt no trace of the cold that had been gnawing at her every limb.

"That amulet is very old," Velma said, no trace of fury in her voice now. "It was made by my people and it possesses a powerful protective magic. I'm glad to see you have taken care of it and the animals it represents. In turn it has taken care of you."

Was risking her own life to save Dante the reason Velma had saved her?

Flora opened her mouth to ask Velma whether she had really been the spiritualist who had given her the amulet, but she was interrupted by the approach of Kaya and Mr Avery.

They were climbing out of their kayaks and on to the ice beside a very damp but very alive Dante. Kaya grabbed Dante and held him close, checking him over for any injuries, stroking his little wet head. He looked very shaken and nestled close into Kaya's neck.

"Oh, my poor balloon!" cried Mr Avery.

He ran over to the wreckage of his balloon, straight past Velma and several mermaids, who watched him curiously. It appeared that he could not see the magical beings either.

The goddess returned to her throne. The polar bears padded back over and settled down on either side of her.

"Polar bear!" Flora ticced, the word jumping out of her.

One of the polar bears lazily glanced over at her.

Velma held her hand out to Flora. In it sat the huge gleaming pearl.

"You can ask anything about the past or the future," she said. "You may only ask it one question about the past, present or future. But it must be the *right* question."

Flora took it from her, awestruck. It was beautiful and very heavy. She gazed into its polished surface. What question should she ask it?

Before she could decide, a muffled noise came from the balloon wreckage nearby. Beside the broken basket was a large pool of the brightly coloured balloon material, which had settled over the crash site like a layer of fresh snow. The balloon material rustled as something struggled out from under it.

Mr Avery gave a shout as Lord Granville emerged, dishevelled, with torn clothing and his moustache pointing in odd angles. With a growl, he lunged forward, snatching the pearl out of Flora's hands.

"No! Give it ba—"

But before Flora could finish her sentence, he

was already asking the pearl a question.

"Show me the future. Show me the best way to become even richer," Lord Granville growled at the pearl, his eyes widening with excited greed.

Velma looked at him coldly. "That is the wrong question," she said.

With that, a narwhal rose out of the water beside them. It swept its unicorn-like horn under Granville's feet so that he lost his footing and fell

with a great splash into the water. The pearl rolled across the ice and stopped at Flora's feet.

"Now it is your turn," Velma said to her.

Glancing nervously at her friends, who nodded encouragingly at her, Flora bent down and picked up the heavy pearl.

She stared into its pearlescent surface. It was tempting to look into the past and see her mother . . . She looked up at Velma, who was watching her with such an expression that Flora knew she could sense the confusion burning inside her. Flora shook her head. Then she repeated the head shake as a tic. Her mother was dead. Seeing her would be the most wonderful thing in the world . . . but it would not bring her back. Nelly could still have her parents, alive and safe at home with her, if she asked the pearl where they were.

"Show me the location of Nelly's parents. Where did they go?" she whispered.

Velma nodded approvingly. Flora realised that it had been a test. The mystic pearl would have been taken from her, like it had been from Lord Granville, had she used her question selfishly.

Suddenly, something bright and shining shot out of the pearl and soared into the sky above them. It hung impossibly in the air for a moment, then burst like a magnificent firework display. The sky was filled with streaks of green and purple.

Flora gasped in wonder. "The Northern Lights!"

They watched, awestruck, as the colours danced across the sky. If only she had her paints! Flora thought about her father back in London and how she wished he could see them too. She had

come very close to never seeing him again, and the thought sent a shudder down her spine.

Slowly, the gleam on the pearl's surface began to form into an image. The pearl showed her a very basic-looking camp. A cave had been hung with a walrus-skin door and a small fire crackled just inside it. Beside the fire was a woman covered with furs. She looked so much like Nelly that Flora was sure it had to be her mother.

Then the woman began to sing. The beautiful music was so familiar that it made Flora's heart glow. All this time the whale amulet had been carrying Nelly's mother's voice. The melody echoed around the cave, just as it had in the ice caves for Flora.

As Nelly's mother sang, a man put his arm round her and led her to the cave entrance, where he pointed to the glowing Northern Lights. She lay her head on his shoulder and together they looked up into the sky where a beautiful collection of stars shone among the magical colours.

"Those stars . . ." murmured Kaya. "That constellation is called Cetus. Also known as the Whale."

The constellation Kaya pointed out was low in the sky, just visible above the mountain Nelly's parents were using for shelter.

Flora's heart leapt. Her mother's message rang through her head once more. *Follow the whale.*

She looked up at the beautiful colours streaking through the sky above them, excitement growing. There! Far off in the distance she could see the constellation twinkling above a craggy mountain.

She turned to the others. "I know where Nelly's parents are!"

One of Velma's polar bears left their place at her side and approached Flora and her friends. Flora's heart started to pound. Was it going to attack? But it lowered its head.

"My bear will take you there," said Velma.

Just then, Lord Granville heaved himself out of the water and on to the ice. "I'm sick of this place, I'm sick of being cold and I'm sick of ice! Someone take me back to camp!" he groaned.

"We should *all* go back to camp," said Kaya, giving him a disgusted look. "Lavinia and Pavan will be worried about us."

Then Flora smiled as an idea crept into her mind. "Mr Avery, would you mind taking Lord Granville back to camp using our kayaks?"

Lord Granville grimaced at the idea, but Mr Avery bounced on his heels.

"Oh, that's a spiffing idea! And while we travel, I'd like to have a little word with Lord Granville about respecting other people's property." He gave a look that could almost be stern if his face weren't so good-natured. "But how will you get back without any boats?"

"Oh," said Flora, giving the enchanted polar bears a grin, "I think we'll be all right."

As Lord Granville stalked past Kaya, Dante popped out of her coat with a squeak.

"Dante, my little chap, come here. Come to Daddy," cooed Lord Granville, opening his arms to the ferret.

Dante climbed down Kaya's coat and began to scurry across the ice towards Lord Granville.

Halfway there he paused and glanced back at Kaya, but he shook his tiny head and leapt into Lord Granville's arms, chattering away to him.

There was a sad look in Kaya's eyes as they watched Mr Avery and Lord Granville paddle out of the lagoon. It was as if she were hoping Dante would appear at Lord Granville's shoulder and look back at her.

One of Velma's polar bears crouched lower to the ground to allow the remaining two friends to climb on to its back. Flora wasn't sure how to hold on; would it hurt to grab its fur? She decided to grip its beautiful seashell collar instead. With great huffing grunts, the polar bear rose to its feet.

The bear began to lope along the ice, but Flora couldn't see a way out of the lagoon except for the watery caves. How were they going to get out?

The bear seemed to know. With enormously big bounding steps, it started to run – straight at an icy wall!

The ice shattered as the bear leapt through it. Without breaking its stride they galloped in the direction of the camp.

"Whee!" cried Flora. This was even better than travelling by dog sled!

# Chapter Thirteen

Flora held tightly on to the enchanted bear's beautiful collar nestled safely in its shaggy white fur as they rushed across the icy plain. It was amazing! The wind whipped past them, whirling in Flora's hair, but she crouched low to be shielded by the bear's massive head.

Soon the bear slowed to a padding pace. Ahead of them, Flora could just about see round the bear's head to make out the camp. The tent was lit from inside with a warm comforting glow.

As they approached, Kaya's dogs began to howl. From a safe distance, the polar bear stopped and lowered its head to the ground to allow the pair to climb off. Flora wished she could introduce her friends to the bear, but without magical amulets like the ones she and Kaya had Lavinia and Pavan wouldn't be able to see it, just as they hadn't been able to see the rainforest spirits on Isla Panacea.

Flora looked up at Kaya, who was giving the bear a scratch behind the ear. There was something very comforting in the knowledge that Kaya had seen Velma and the mermaids too. It was wonderful being able to share this magical gift with another person.

As they approached the camp, she began to

hear the voices of her friends. It made her heart swell with joy to know that they were both safe!

"Lavinia?" came the worried voice of Pavan from within the tent. "I think I can hear something outside . . ."

"Get behind me, Pavan!" cried Lavinia.

"No, it's all right!" called Flora as she popped her head inside the tent. "It's just me."

Lavinia sighed with relief. "Oh, thank goodness you're OK!"

Pavan ran over and gave Flora a big hug, then turned and hugged Kaya as she too entered the tent.

"Have one of these," said Pavan, giving them each one of his fruity inventions.

Flora felt better with some food in her belly.

"So . . ." said Pavan, "what happened?"

"We met Velma! She was . . . a little frightening," Flora admitted. "But she let us use the pearl and now we know where Nelly's parents are!"

"What happened to the balloon?" asked Lavinia anxiously. "Did you see Mr Avery? Was he all right?"

They could hear the distant sound of footsteps approaching.

"I'll let Mr Avery fill you in," she said.

A few moments later, Lord Granville threw open the flaps of the tent and stalked in as if he owned the place. Close behind him came Mr Avery. Lavinia rushed forward as if to hug him, then seemed to grow shy and ended up awkwardly sticking her hand out for a handshake.

"I don't quite know what happened; it was all a

bit of a blur," said Mr Avery, grinning at Lavinia. "But I do know that none of us would be here without Flora."

"Oh, congratulations, what a lovely story, well done, Miss Goody Two-Shoes," Lord Granville said in a sarcastic voice as he rummaged through the supplies at the back of the tent.

"What should we do about him?" whispered Lavinia, gesturing towards Lord Granville.

"I'll stay with him," volunteered Kaya. "He took a nasty fall in that hot-air balloon and he's been in the freezing waters. Taking care of him is the right thing to do, even if he's not the nicest patient."

"Well, that leaves the rest of us for the rescue mission!" said Mr Avery, bouncing on his heels with excitement.

Flora smiled at his enthusiasm. She couldn't blame Lavinia for taking a shine to him!

Together they harnessed the dogs to their sleds, then Flora and Pavan climbed on to one dog sled, while Mr Avery helped Lavinia on to the second.

Velma's magical polar bear was waiting for them just outside camp, though only Flora could see it. The Whale constellation glittered in the sky above them. Somewhere, under those stars, were Nelly's parents!

"This way!" cried Flora, following the polar bear, her heart pounding with excitement.

It was comforting seeing the galloping figure of Velma's polar bear ahead of them as they crossed the unforgiving landscape towards the constellation and the mountain below. She could hear her whale necklace singing over the sound of the fierce, rushing wind.

After a while, though, Flora's excitement faded as the cold winds and the exhaustion of the long journey took their toll. She was beginning to feel discouraged when—

"Look!" shouted Pavan.

From behind a large iceberg a shipwreck revealed itself. The bear began to slow down as they approached it, and they brought their sleds to a halt.

"It's the *Discovery*," whispered Lavinia. "The Nortons' ship."

It was eerily quiet, and Flora began to wonder if she had mistaken what she saw in the pearl. Had Nelly's parents perished with their doomed ship? Was she about to find them here, rather than at the mountain?

She climbed on to the ice. "Hello?" she called nervously up at the ship, half frightened of getting a response.

"It looks like they got stuck in the ice, just like the *Endeavour*," said Pavan, walking to the front of the ship.

There was a simple rope ladder hanging over the side of the ship. Without really knowing what she was going to do, Flora stepped on the first rung.

"Be careful!" called Lavinia, as Flora began her climb up the side of the massive ship.

When she climbed on to the deck, a shiver of fear ran through her and she scrunched her nose over and over, unable to get rid of the funny feeling that made her tic. It was as if her body was telling her something was very wrong.

The ship was very, very still. It looked as if it

were ready to sail at any moment; the ropes were still knotted, the crates of equipment waiting to be opened. The only thing missing was the crew.

Nervously, Flora made her way towards the captain's quarters. But as she gripped the door handle, something inside told her to stop. She decided to peer through the window instead.

Through the warped glass, she saw an eerie scene. The captain's dining table was set for an extravagant dinner. It looked so appealing except . . . it was all dusted with frost. Above the table the beautiful crystal chandelier was dripping with icicles.

She stared at the table and wondered where the crew had gone. It was as if they had just . . . disappeared. It truly was a ghost ship.

"Come on," came Lavinia's echoing voice from

below. "They're not here."

Flora looked towards the mountain she had seen in the pearl's surface. They weren't far from it now. But now she had seen the ship and its chilling atmosphere, she felt less sure of herself and her vision. What if Nelly's parents weren't there any more?

With one last glance at the frozen dining room, she climbed down the ladder and made her way back to her friends.

"What did you see?" Pavan asked excitedly.

Flora shook her head. She felt quite uncomfortable about the ghost ship, and she wasn't quite sure how to put that feeling into words.

The polar bear padded onwards, as they climbed on to their sleds again, moving past the shipwreck and on towards the mountain.

The unsettled cloud that had formed in Flora's mind began to clear as they approached a cave nestled into the mountain's rugged, stony base. She could hear the sound of singing – and now it wasn't just coming from her whale necklace.

Could it be? Was this the cave she had seen in the surface of the pearl?

Flora's breath caught as they entered. Inside the cave, sheltered from the worst weather, was a basic camp. There was the walrus-skin door. By a small fire a woman covered with furs rubbed her eyes and shook the shoulder of the man sitting beside her.

"Darling, I'm hallucinating," she said. "I can see people."

The man just stared at them in amazement, his

mouth gaping open and closed like a fish.

"It's not a dream," Flora reassured them. "Nelly sent us to rescue you."

Mrs Norton cautiously reached out and touched Flora's arm, as if to check whether she was really there. Then she took her in a tight hug, whispering,

"My darling Nelly. What a clever girl."

Flora knew that the hug was meant for Nelly, but she closed her eyes and imagined her own mother's arms round her with a smile.

"It feels like magic that you're here," Mr Norton finally said in an awed whisper.

"Well, there might have been a bit of magic involved," said Pavan, grinning and nudging Flora.

"How did you find us?" asked Mrs Norton.

"It's a long story," said Lavinia, guiding them to the sleds outside. "But it'll be a long voyage home, and we can tell you everything then."

Flora could hardly believe her eyes when, weeks later, they finally sailed up the River Thames. After the desolate icy landscape of the Arctic, the city of London seemed so busy and colourful! As they approached the docks, she spotted Nelly and her governess anxiously waiting for them, along with Flora's father and Mrs Fairweather. She called out to them and waved excitedly.

"Nelly!" cried Mrs Norton as she ran down the

gangplank, sweeping Nelly into her arms. "My own Nelly!"

Dr Norton was close behind, gathering them both up, as they all began to cry. "I promise we'll never leave you again. Ever!" he said.

Flora felt tears welling up in her own eyes as she threw herself at her father and held on tightly. It had been a long, difficult adventure, but it had all been worth it.

"Where's Lavinia?" asked Flora's father.

"She's with Mr Avery," said Pavan. "They haven't stopped talking since they came aboard!"

They all turned to see Lavinia and Mr Avery walking down the gangplank arm in arm. They approached and Lavinia introduced him to Flora's father. Mr Avery shook his hand heartily.

"I'm sorry about your hot-air balloon," said Flora.

"Oh, not to worry!" Mr Avery chuckled. "I'm already planning another hot-air balloon expedition, and this time Miss West will be coming along too." He gave her a beaming smile, which she returned.

"Except maybe the next voyage won't be to the Arctic," Lavinia suggested with a laugh.

"Yes," said Mr Avery with a serious expression.

"I was thinking perhaps a honeymoon . . ."

Lavinia laughed and blushed bright red.

As they all chatted, Flora looked over to Nelly and her parents. Nelly's mother could hardly stop cuddling and kissing her daughter! Flora's heart ached a little, thinking about how much she missed her own mother. But she knew she had done the right thing in using the pearl's magic to find Mr and Mrs Norton. She looked up at her father, her heart absolutely full of love, and knew how happy she was to be back with him again.

Flora took off the whale necklace and stared down at it, thinking of the spiritualist, who might – or might not – have been Velma. Had her mother really given her that message? She took a deep breath and decided that it didn't matter. Either way, the amulet had protected her and guided her, just as Velma had told her it would. And now she was safely back home.

Flora approached the edge of the dock, where the river lapped. She dropped the amulet into the water as an offering to Velma. She hoped it would be carried out to sea, and that the sea goddess would eventually receive the offering.

"Thank you, Velma," she whispered. "For keeping me and my friends safe. I promise to always honour the creatures of the sea."

She stared down, watching the necklace sink. It might have been her imagination, but for a moment, Flora was sure she saw a flash of the Northern Lights and the swirl of a mermaid tail just beneath the water's surface.

## The End

# Isabella Harcourt

lives with a very large cat called Freddie Witchfinder. She loves to write about interesting people having fantastic adventures! Bella has Tourette's syndrome just like Flora Stormer. She hopes that everyone reading about Flora will see that adventures are for everybody, and having tics will not stop you from having a wonderful life.

Her favourite things always sneak themselves into her writing, so look out for mentions of plants, pirates and magic! Oh, and her cat Freddie Witchfinder, of course, and his two best cat friends Hooch and Pod!

# Hannah McCaffery

has always been an illustrator and storyteller from a young age, when she would fill dozens of sketchbooks with characters and stories.

She went on to study Illustration for Children's Publishing at Glyndwr University before working as an in-house illustrator and designer for a number of companies.

She finds her inspiration from the characters she comes across (mainly dogs) each day and from rambling through the beautiful Welsh countryside. Hannah has always believed that illustrations should depict emotion so that you can really feel involved in the story and she strives to deliver that in her work.

# Dear Reader,

When I was about seven years old, my nose started to twitch like a bunny whenever I was nervous or upset. Lots of people noticed and told me to stop or even laughed at me, but I couldn't help it! It felt like an itch that I just couldn't scratch. As I got older, that funny itchy feeling moved around, making me click my fingers or kick my feet, and sometimes I would shout words out of the blue. And what's worse, the more I worried about it, the more often it happened.

Now I'm grown up, I know that those were called tics, and that I have a condition called Tourette's syndrome. Just like the stars Billie Eilish and Lewis Capaldi – and, of course, Flora Stormer! I don't use the words "Tourette's syndrome" in Flora's books, because they are based in a historical setting when the term wasn't used.

I've tried to use my own experiences with Tourette's when writing about Flora. Everybody is different though, and it might be that my tics are not the same as other people who have the condition. Medicine wasn't available to treat Tourette's syndrome in Flora's time, but today it is. I take medicine to help me manage the condition, whereas other people manage it in different ways.

Having Tourette's isn't easy; in fact, sometimes it's very difficult. But I've found that people understand more than you think they will, and that things become easier when you talk to someone you love about how you're feeling.

Isabella Harcourt

Don't miss Flora's first adventure

FLORA STORMER
and the Golden Lotus

Flora trod carefully through the jungle, excitement stirring in her belly. She pushed past thick vines which hung from colossal trees and dodged the reaching leaves and flowers of countless tropical plants, knowing her destination couldn't be much further.

The canopy above her was alive with the echoing sounds of the creatures that called the jungle home. Bright birds whistled and sang as they swooped through the trees, their colourful feathers flashing against the green leaves. In the distance, a family of monkeys called to one another as they swung from branch to branch.

She was nearly there.

But as she pushed one more branch aside, she found herself teetering on the edge of a huge and unexpected ravine. She stumbled in surprise, one foot slipping and sending mud skittering down into the abyss far, far below. The dizzying drop made her head spin for a second before she managed to grab on to a vine to steady herself.

Suddenly, a low growl behind her made her turn around very . . . slowly . . . A jaguar stood behind her, its eyes staring, its teeth bared. It took a step towards her, but Flora thought fast! She grabbed tightly on to a hanging vine and swung across the ravine—

"There you are!" Flora's father poked his head around the door. His dark hair stuck up in strange places like he had forgotten to brush it, and his brown eyes twinkled with a thousand ideas. He gave a broad smile at the sight of Flora sitting at her easel. "Time to get ready."

Flora quickly began to pack up her paints. She could feel the daydream slowly dissolving away in her mind. The jungle, and the jaguar, would have to wait.

"Oh, this is wonderful," her father said, leaning close to inspect her painting of a hibiscus flower. The real flower sat in front of them, its petals the colour of a setting sun. "How well you've captured the details . . . those oranges and yellows . . ."

"Didn't you say we needed to leave?" Flora said, laughing.

"Oh! Quite so, quite so . . ." Her father straightened, but still looked lost in thought. He clapped his hands. "Yes, right. I shall meet you in the hallway in five minutes. We have a big day ahead of us!"

Alone, Flora tried to rub the paint from her hands. As it did after every conversation, Flora's mind sifted through the words she'd just heard, then offered them back to her in strange combinations that seemed to soothe an itch in her brain. *Orange details. Five orange minutes. Big day, big day.*

She said "big day" out loud and clapped her hands, but it wasn't on purpose. Sometimes she did and said things without meaning to. Her father called these things her tics.

As she got ready to go, Flora saw a new smudge of paint on her dress. *I don't have time for this*, she thought as she frantically tried to clean it. It was times like these when she desperately missed her mother, who had died when she was five. She had been kind – and *very* organised. Her father always said she looked like her mother, with light brown hair, prominent front teeth and freckles, and the thought always made Flora smile. She wished her mother could have been there for her father's important day: giving his lecture to the Royal Scientific Society.

Flora hoped she could keep her tics under control. They were always worse when she was anxious, and as they walked through the busy streets to the Royal Society, Flora had never been so anxious in her life.

"Tell me about your trip to Isla Panacea," she said to her father, hoping to distract herself.

The urge to tic rose up and she clicked her tongue twice.

He smiled. "Again?"

She grinned back. "Again."

"Well," he began as they crossed a road filled with carriages, "a long time ago, I went on an expedition to the heart of a rainforest on a tiny island—"

**Find out what happens next in**

Look out for more
adventures about
Flora Stormer!

COMING SOON